THE HOTWIFE

&

HER CUCKOLD

BY

AVERY ROWAN

The Hotwife & Her Cuckold

Volume One

By Avery Rowan

First Edition

For up-to-date news on Avery's latest releases, book signing events in your area, and giveaways, follow Avery's newsletter - http://eepurl.com/dCBBwP

FROM THE FRONT SEAT

Dave finished washing the dishes and then checked the time. He had just enough time to get to the mall to pick up his wife, who had told him to be there at closing to help her with her purchases. He'd be there. He would always be there. He did everything Stacy ever asked of him. That, of course, was his place, his role in their marriage. She was the queen, his queen, and him, her humble servant, especially when she was wanting to have her fun. Then, he was more than just her servant. He was her cuckold, there to provide whatever she or her lover needed, when they needed it.

Dave dried his hands, tossing the towel on the counter when he finished. Grabbing his keys, he headed out the door to the van, cell phone in his other hand as he stepped out into the night. He was thinking it was going to be a quiet night, but he had the thought a little too soon as his phone dinged with a text notification. He took a deep breath, somehow knowing what he would find when he looked at it.

He wasn't disappointed. *I need you to prepare the van for me. You will be picking me up along with someone else. You will open the side door, and you will not say anything until I allow you to speak.* He should have known she would have one of her many lovers there. He sighed, but at the same time, his cock started to harden in his pants. He was about to shove his phone into his pocket when the notification sound dinged again. *And do not be late.*

He wouldn't be late.

A year ago, they had bought one of those vans where all the seats folded down into the floorboard and out of sight just for such occasions. Stacy used their van quite often for such encounters, and Dave didn't know why he even bothered keeping the middle seats up anymore. Opening the passenger side door, he flipped the middle seat down and tucked it into the floorboard, straightening the mat out over the compartment to hide the hinges. He then quickly did the same thing to the middle seat on the driver's side, leaving the center of the van completely open for whatever his wife and her lover wanted. Dave wondered who the lucky man was who would be banging his wife tonight. She had about three men she met regularly for her own private fun, sometimes making Dave watch, quite often making him clean up after her lover had left. She loved making Dave watch her being ravished by another man, seeing another cock driving into her, bringing her to orgasmic ecstasy. Seeing her give herself to someone other than him. Truth be told, he loved it as well, which is why they were living the life they were. Dave had no qualms about where they were in their sex life. Stacy loved him, would never leave him, but she needed other cocks, other men to do things to her he couldn't do because his cock just wasn't big enough to fill her the way she loved to be filled. The whole thing made her pussy drip and his cock hard as hell. No matter who she fucked during the day, she was always in his bed at night.

Once he had prepared the van the way Stacy desired for her little trysts, Dave hopped behind the wheel and started the engine. Time to see who his wife was fucking tonight.

The night was dark, a perfect cloak for whatever Stacy had planned since they would be outside. He pulled into the parking lot of the mall, turning left and heading to the largest department store on the far end. His wife never did anything small, from shopping trips to the size of her lovers.

When Dave approached the entrance to the department store, he opened the side door by pushing a button and waited, giving the rearview mirror a slight adjustment so he could see into the back where the action would soon be taking place. Stacy came out of the store, arms loaded down with bags, followed by a tall man with bronze skin and a confident swagger, his eyes glued to Stacy's ass, her dress hugging her hips like an extra set of hands. Dave couldn't blame the man. Stacy had the perfect rear, curvy with a lot of bounce when she walked that drew eyes to her. Dave had watched her lovers take handfuls of her ass as they pummeled her pussy from behind, gripping her tight as they pulled her back and forth onto their cocks. The sight never ceased to make his cock hard.

Dave opened the back door on the van for his wife's many bags. The man with her—Bryan, Dave recalled was his name— slid into the van as Stacy put her bags into the back. Dave kept silent as he glanced at the other man through the rearview mirror.

There was no greeting, no friendliness. It wasn't required after all. Tonight, Dave was a mere chauffeur, and Bryan was the man about to fuck Stacy. All they expected of Dave was to drive them around or find a dark spot somewhere and park while they got lost in their adventure.

Stacy closed the back of the van and then walked around and got in, ignoring her husband as well. The fact that she didn't even say hello to him made his cock twitch as he watched her slide into the back seat with her lover, her hand grazing the crotch of Bryan's pants. As soon as she was sitting down, her attention swallowed up by the thick-bodied lover beside her, Dave hit the button to close the side door, slipped the van into drive, and pulled away from the storefront. He could hear the two of them whispering as he took the curve out of the parking lot and onto one of the side streets behind the mall. He knew where a closed business was near the mall and would park there while his wife and her lover had their fun.

Darting his gaze to the mirror, Dave saw Stacy working the button and zipper on Bryan's pants, the man's hand around her neck, massaging it. As soon as his thick, dark cock was out, Bryan gripped Stacy's neck and shoved her mouth down onto his manhood. "That's a good slut," he said. "Get my cock nice and ready for that cunt of yours."

Stacy had time to giggle once before the other man stuffed her mouth was stuffed with his thick rod. Dave felt his own cock harden as he watched the giant cock slip between his wife's lush red lips, disappearing inch by inch as she took the length of him.

Bryan slid his hand up her neck and into her hair where he took a giant handful, gripping it tight as he forced her head up and down, fucking her face as he leaned back in the seat, looking down at the blond blowing him. Dave could hear the slurp sounds coming from his wife as she sucked the man's cock, taking the abuse to her mouth as he shoved her face down onto him harder and faster. How Stacy wasn't choking on the man's thick shaft, Dave had no idea.

Turning his attention back to the road, Dave found the entrance to the business he had in mind and drove around to the back and out of sight. Parking under a large oak, the branches providing a blanket of sorts from onlookers who might wander around the side of the building, he slipped the car into park and left the engine running. He was sure the two in the back would need the air-conditioning before the night was over. Then, Dave settled back in his seat, his gaze glued to the rearview mirror while he rubbed his cock through his pants.

Bryan groaned as he shoved Stacy down on his cock, and then, without warning, gripped her hair tighter and yanked her face away from his thick shaft, shoving her off the seat and down onto the floorboard of the van. "Turn around," he ordered.

Stacy obeyed, turning on her knees so she faced the front of the van. Dave saw the lustful grin on her face as she caught his eyes in the rearview mirror, and he knew her pussy was dripping.

"Show me that ass," Bryan said. "Slow and tempting."

Stacy bit her lower lip as she gripped the sides of her dress, very slowly pulling the fabric up her thighs and over her ass until Bryan could see her peach thong tucked between her ass cheeks. "Is this what you wanted?" she asked, swinging her ass back and forth slightly.

"God, yes," Bryan said. He leaned forward and shoved Stacy down onto her hands, putting her in a perfect doggy-style position, her dress still gripped in her hands. He then pulled her panties to the side as he shoved two fingers into her pussy, driving them in deep and making her gasp out loud as she rocked forward slightly. "And this is what you want, isn't it? Something crammed into your nasty little cunt."

"Oh, god, yes!" she cried out. "I want to be filled. I want your cock, Bryan. Please, give it to me. Please, use me!" She arched her back as he finger-fucked her, shoving his fingers in and out of her so hard Dave could hear her juices and the sound of slapping flesh from Bryan's knuckles on her pussy. She groaned out loud as the van rocked with how hard she was being fingered. "Oh! God, Bryan, yes!"

Then Bryan yanked his fingers from her soaking sex and smacked her on the ass. "Lift that ass up here and fuck me. Now!"

Dave watched as his wife scooted back, lifting her ass in the air until her slit was hovering over Bryan's massive cock. That thickness, that length is what she craved that Dave knew he couldn't give her. He could only watch as other men stretched his wife's slit wide before their well-hung shafts. Bryan held Stacy's pale hips as she lowered herself onto his dark pole, her pussy swallowing every thick inch of his superior manhood. She groaned as she settled down on him, and then she started bouncing her ass up and down, her pink slit sliding along the cock she had impaled herself on as Bryan gripped her hips tightly.

Bryan fixed his gaze on Stacy's ass, while Dave couldn't look away from the image in the rearview mirror, rubbing his cock faster through his pants as he stared.

"That's it, you little slut," Bryan practically growled at the woman fucking him. "Take that cock. Ride it, you sweet piece of ass."

And that's what Stacy was to these men, just a piece of ass, a willing pussy to stick their large cocks in and get off. They used her for the short time they had her and then walked off never thinking of her again until they needed a wet cunt once more. Stacy was always that wet cunt.

7

Her cries filled the van as she bounced, her tits swaying within her dress. Dave couldn't take his eyes away from the sight as he slipped his own cock from the confines of his jeans and into his eager hand. Gripping it, he started jerking off as he watched his wife fuck her lover.

Bryan pushed Stacy off his cock and back onto her knees, shoving her forward as he slid off the seat, his pants sliding down to his ankles. He pushed her forward until her head was between the two front seats, and then he knelt behind her, grabbing her hips, and thrusting his cock deep into her until his heavy balls slapped at her clit. She cried out, moaning and whimpering as Bryan drove into her, pounding her so hard Dave could hear her juices as they coated the man's cock.

Bryan snaked a hand up her back, pulling her dress up higher and baring more of her flesh. He then gripped her hair and yanked her head back, her throat stretched as he rammed in and out of her pussy.

Dave looked over as his wife's mouth stretched wide with her moans, begging Bryan to fuck her like a little slut, *his* little slut. She then glanced at her husband and smirked. "Fuck me like a real man would."

Dave felt his cock throb, snatched an old fast food napkin beside him, and shot his load into it as his groan mixed with his wife's, his gaze riveted to her as she took the fucking.

His orgasm was what she needed to break through to her own, her body tightening as she screamed, shoving her ass back onto Bryan's cock, taking him all the way inside of her as she shuddered. Bryan kept fucking her as she turned into a cascading wave of pleasure, her pussy sucking his cock like her mouth had done just a few moments ago.

Once her orgasm subsided, Bryan thrust into her one last time, and then, he jerked his cock out of her pussy as ropes of hot cum sprayed along her back. His heavy breathing made his chest rise and fall as he pushed his balls against her ass until he had emptied himself onto her back and ass, the streams of cum splattering on her pale flesh.

Dave watched, his cock still in his hand, as the other man finished off on his wife. She looked back over her shoulder at the bronze man, grinning as she bounced her eyebrows at him. "God, that was hot," she said. "I needed that."

Bryan eased away from her, moving so he could sit back on the seat, his pants still at his ankles. "Oh, so did I. Sorry about the mess."

Her grin grew. "Oh, that isn't a problem." She turned to Dave, calling his name.

He knew that was his cue and pushed the button that opened the side door. He then opened his door and slid out into the night. As he walked around to her side of the van, he slid his cock back into his pants and zipped up. Stacy slid out of the van, her dress still gathered high around her waist. When Dave reached her, she bent over and shoved her ass out at him, holding herself up with her palms on the floorboard of the van, her dress draped over her back. She wiggled her ass at him.

Dave placed a hand on each of her hips as he stared down at the cum sprayed across her ass and dripping down her crack. Out of the corner of his eye, he saw Bryan watching him, the man's cock still hard and coated with Stacy's passion. With a deep breath, Dave leaned over and ran his tongue up his wife's ass crack, the cum pooling on his tongue as he lapped it up, swallowing it as he did. He ran his tongue up and down each side of her ass crack, her panties bunched to the side and out of the way still, tonguing her tight asshole as well, until satisfied her backdoor slit was clean. Then, he ran his tongue over the rest of her ass and lower back, making sure to get every drop of Bryan's cum, cleaning his wife after her lover had used her.

When Dave was sure she was clean, he stood and walked back over to the driver's door, sliding back into his seat. No words, no thank you, no good boy. He did his job and now could taste Bryan's cum on his lips. His cock throbbed again.

Returning his gaze back to the rearview mirror, he saw the other man smirk at him, and then Bryan returned his attention back to Stacy as she slid back into the van, her dress now snug in place. She took her spot next to Bryan and leaned over, using her mouth to clean his semi-hard cock. Bryan placed a hand on her head as he stared at Dave in the mirror.

Pushing the button, Dave closed the side door, and then slipped the van into reverse. Once the cleaning happened, he knew the night was over. It was time to return Bryan to his own car and take Stacy home.

Back at the mall, Dave opened the side door again, watching as the others slid out and back into the night. Stacy wrapped her hands around Bryan's neck as she leaned in to kiss him, her lush lips pressed hard against his as their bodies ground together. Bryan slid a hand down to Stacy's ass, lifting her dress until her pale cheeks were visible to anyone who wanted to watch, and squeezed it, leaving marks where his nails dug into her flesh.

Dave slid out of the driver's seat and walked around to open her door while she stood embraced with her latest lover.

Breaking the kiss, Stacy grinned at the darker man. "Don't wait too long to call me again."

Bryan finished zipping his pants as he nodded. "Don't worry. I won't. That ass is worth coming back for."

Stacy ran a hand up the length of Bryan's cock, now tucked out of sight. "Good to hear." She then leaned in and kissed him again. "Until then." She turned and slid into the passenger seat of the van, Dave closing the door behind her.

She didn't even look at Bryan as they pulled away. Instead, she leaned over the center console and took Dave's hand in hers, one hand sliding up his chest to his chin. Dave slowed the van as she turned his head to face her, leaned in and kissed him, her tongue licking around the inside of his mouth. "God, you taste good." She giggled as she plopped back in her seat. "Now, take me home and ram that cock of yours into my pussy."

Dave grinned. "Yes, my dear." He knew it would be a long night with him down between his wife's thighs, lapping at her drenched pussy. Fucking other men only made her hornier, rather than satisfying her itch, a side effect for which Dave was quite glad. "It will be my pleasure." Then, he looked back in the rearview mirror at the now empty seat. Yeah, he definitely needed to just leave the center seats tucked away.

HIS BOOTY-CALL WIFE

Missy slipped her robe over her bare shoulders as she left the bedroom, her hair still damp from her shower. She could hear her husband, Nick, in the kitchen putting the finishing touches of dinner together. He was such a good boy, doing everything he was told and never bothering to argue. Ever since Missy caught him jerking off to a video of two black men taking a white woman as her husband watched from a chair beside the bed, Missy had made sure that Nick knew his new role in the house. Oh, he had balked at first, saying the videos meant nothing, and he had just stumbled across them. However, a quick glance at his search history on his laptop told her—and him—that he had been truly busted in his fantasies, fantasies that Missy fully intended to make a reality. If this is what her husband wanted, then this was damn well what he would get. She only wished she had known about his little perversion years ago. *So many wasted cocks I could have had by now*, she thought with a sigh. "Don't forget to sweep the floor when you're done," she said as she entered the kitchen. "I hate walking on dirty floors. Makes my feet feel all gross."

"Yes, love," Nick said as he glanced up at her and smiled. "Did your shower feel good?"

"Lonely, but good," she replied with a dramatic sigh. "I could have used some hard-bodied stud in there bending me over and drilling into me from behind." She then glanced at him, a smirk on her face. "Too bad I'm stuck with a man who can only watch."

"Hey, I like fucking you, too," Nick said as he reached for the broom. "Just because we started this path, doesn't mean I want to give up everything else."

Missy walked over to him and patted his cheek. "Perhaps, you don't want to give up everything else, but I just couldn't have that small cock of yours in my hungry pussy now that I know I can have bigger and better. Your job is to watch, serve, and clean up. If you're lucky, I'll permit you the relief of jerking your tiny dick off, but only once my lovers and I are finished with you."

He looked sullen, his lips turned down in a pout as he dropped his gaze to the floor. She didn't feel sorry for him, however. She stopped feeling sorry for him the moment she saw how hard he got as another man bent her over and drove his cock into her, making her cry out in ecstasy as she surrendered to every whim her lover had. Nick might appear miserable and hurt when the sex was over, but as soon as the fun began, he became lost in his role as cuckold, his gaze locked onto his wife as she took cocks in all of her holes.

Missy leaned in and kissed his cheek. "Aw, now, don't be like that. This is what you wanted after all, remember? You begged for this, to be a little cuckold while I found cocks that could please me." She reached down and stroked his flaccid

15

member, giving it a little squeeze as she did. "You're only getting what you really wanted." She kissed his cheek again. "Now, why don't you pour us each a glass of wine and meet me in the living room. We'll watch some TV before bed." She patted his arm as she turned and walked away, leaving him standing there holding the broom. Life had become so much better since she found out her husband yearned to be a cuckold.

~ ~ ~ ~ ~

Nick took Missy's wine glass from her hand as he leaned forward on the couch, the movie they were watching now over. "That was a good show," he said as he stood to his feet. He then turned and glanced down at Missy, a glint in his eye. "Maybe you'd like me to entertain you in some other way." He bounced his eyebrows as he stood there, hoping she would take him up on his offer.

Missy had been right earlier when she said that he craved to be her cuckold. He loved watching her being fucked by someone with a much bigger cock than him, the pleasure she derived from it as they speared into her, making her cry out with pleasure as she came over and over. Still, that didn't mean he didn't like to fuck her as well. Once in a while, she would permit him to put his small cock inside of her, but she always made him eat her out afterward because she never came from his inadequate dick. He had grown so used to the taste of his own cum that when she started making him clean up after her other lovers, he didn't balk, but dove right between her legs and licked up her juices and ate the cum out of her pussy. He hoped tonight Missy would permit him between her legs if even out of pity for him.

A knock at the front door, however, told him his plans were not going to happen. At least, not right then. He groaned as he set the glasses back onto the coffee table, glancing back at Missy. "Are we expecting company?"

Missy shrugged. "You never know these days, do you? I'm just as surprised as you."

Nick nodded as he turned to answer the door. It was his job after all. If Missy was expecting someone, she would have told him, rubbing it in as she made him clean her and shave her in preparation for her lover. Another one of his jobs. She loved making him pick out her outfits and bathe her for another man. No, Missy didn't know who was at their front door. Whoever was knocking that late at night had kept their visit a secret, which probably meant they hadn't even known they would be showing up themselves. Nick felt a mixture of elation at what it could be and disappointment that his night alone with Missy had been cut short.

When he opened the door, two tall, muscular black men stood there, dressed as if they had just left a date waiting somewhere. Nick put a smile on his face as he greeted them, knowing who they were, and why they were there. "Hello, Mark. Vince. Kind of late at night, isn't it?"

Mark pushed his way inside, Vince right on his heels. "Evening, Cuck," Mark said. "It's never too late for a booty call."

Turning, Nick noticed Missy shifting on the couch to face the others, a grin spreading across her face. "Well, hello, boys," she said. "What brings you two by tonight?"

Mark and Vince plopped down on each side of her, their arms stretching out along the couch behind her. "Our dates decided they didn't feel like putting out tonight," Vince said as he leaned in and kissed Missy's neck. "So of course, we came to our favorite piece of ass."

Mark glanced over at Nick, who was still standing there watching the three on the couch. Nick's gut clenched at the scene while his cock grew stiff in his pants. "Cuck, go pour us some drinks while we get your wife naked," Mark said.

Missy turned to her husband, a salacious grin on her face. "You heard him, dear. Refreshments for our guests. Looks like we're in for a fun night."

Nick stood there for a moment staring at his wife sandwiched between the more masculine black men, but only for a moment. He knew delay would see he didn't get to watch what was surely about to happen, and he desperately wanted to watch.

As he entered the kitchen, he could hear them laughing and giggling, and he could only imagine what they were doing at that point. He made the drinks quickly so he could return to the living room and the festivities. By the time he made it back, one glass of wine and two whiskey neats in hand, Mark had his pants off and Missy was bent over, her mouth swallowing his thick, dark shaft as she massaged his heavy balls. Vince was caressing her ass, her nightie pulled up to her waist and her panties down at her ankles. They had pulled her tits out of the top of her nightie, and Mark toyed with her swollen nipple as he held her head. Nick walked in and set the glasses on the coffee table, and then moved over to a recliner and sat down. He would not be needed or called upon until the three of them were sated.

Missy bobbed her head up and down on Mark's massive cock, the length more than she could fit down her throat, so she jacked the base off with one hand. Vince leaned over, kissing Missy's pale ass as he slid a hand between her thighs toward her wetness. Nick watched as his wife pushed her rear back toward Vince's hand, opening her legs to his touch. Nick could only stare. These men hadn't called, hadn't texted, didn't even have plans to come over when their night started. Their dates had turned frigid, and so they arrived on his door to fuck his wife, making her their booty call for the evening, a call Missy gladly answered. Now, they had her spread between them as they began to get their rocks off, and Nick could only sit there and watch, watch as his cock continued to harden in his pants.

Mark slid a hand up into Missy's hair, wrapping a handful into his fist as he shoved her face up and down on his cock faster, fucking her face as he watched the back of her head. Nick could hear the slurping noises his wife made with her mouth on the cock she sucked, heard her moans as Vince toyed with her pussy folds. Then Vince turned to face Nick, his lips twisted into a sneer as he shoved his fingers deep into Missy's wetness. She cried out around Mark's cock as she shoved her ass back to meet Vince's fingers, her back arching a little at the feeling that filled her.

"Is your cock getting hard, Cuck?" Vince said as he grinned at Nick as he continued to finger-fuck Missy. "Why don't you take your pitiful cock out so your slut wife can see why she's our booty call. Come on. Let her see that tiny dick of yours and how much you enjoy seeing her be used by two strong black men." Vince continued to mock Nick, taunt him while Vince had his fingers buried into Missy's cunt.

Missy continued to moan around Mark's cock, her body squirming between the two men.

Nick did as Vince ordered, standing and pulling his pants off, his cock—his much smaller cock—springing out in front of him.

Vince laughed at him. "Sit down and watch real men treat your wife the way she should be treated." He started ramming his fingers in and out of Missy's pussy faster, his knuckles obviously pounding into her folds as he just grinned at Nick.

It wasn't new to Nick. Mark and Vince had been here before, fucking Missy, either together or alone. They liked to torment Nick when they did it, make him know he was inferior to their massive manhoods. While Nick hated it, he could not deny how hard the humiliation made his cock. That was why, right then, he sat back down, his cock pointing straight up, and stroked it in front of the other men who were about to fuck his wife.

Mark pulled Missy's mouth off his cock and shoved her toward Vince, turning her so that her ass now faced him. Vince stood, stripping his pants off, and then sat back down, grabbing Missy's head and shoving her down onto his cock. She eagerly opened her mouth and took him deep inside. Mark slid from the couch, dropping behind Missy's ass and lowered his face to her pussy lips, his tongue gliding up her wet slit and back down until he found her swollen pearl. Nick watched as Mark gripped his wife's hips, spreading her ass before him as he tongued her. Missy continued to wiggle on the couch, her head bobbing up and down on Vince's meaty rod as Mark ate her cunt, preparing her for what they would do to her next.

Nick continued to stroke himself as Vince shoved Missy's head down on his cock, the sounds filling their living room. Mark continued to lick Missy's pussy, his fingers digging into her flesh, for a few more minutes, and then stood behind her, his cock at her entrance. He ran his dark hand up her back and the contrast stood out to Nick. Here was this powerful man, strong, muscular, dominant, standing behind Missy, ready to claim her for his once more. "Are you ready, my slut," Mark said, but he didn't wait for an answer. He thrust into her, sinking his cock balls deep into her pussy as he grunted. He pounded in and out of her, his hips slamming into her ass as she continued to suck Vince's cock, groaning around the shaft in her mouth. The sight drove Nick to stroke his cock even faster.

Mark slid his hand up Missy's back and into her hair, taking a fistful and pulling her head back and off Vince's cock. "I think it's time to see how full we can make this little slut," he said. "What do you think, Vince?"

Vince just grinned, his smile making his eyes sparkle with mischief. "I'm ready to sink my cock into her." He grabbed Missy's cheeks, making her look at him. "Do you want it, Missy? Do you want our cocks?"

"Yes!" Missy cried out as Mark kept pounding into her. "Yes, I want them both. Fuck me. Use me. Please!" She kept bouncing back, trying to get Mark's cock into her even deeper as Nick just sat there and watched, his own cock in his hand.

Vince sat up as Mark slid his cock out of Missy's pussy. He then reached out and grabbed Missy's arm, pulling her toward him. "Time to go for a ride, little slut."

Nick watched as his wife straddled Vince, her pale legs wrapping around his darker body. She reached down and grabbed his massive rod, guiding it into her soaking cunt. Nick could hear her moan as she slid down onto it, taking its full length into her pussy. Vince took one of her large breasts in his hand, guiding her nipple to his mouth. Nick watched as the man's tongue swirled around her tight bud, flicking it back and forth before he sucked it into his mouth. Missy moaned as she rode Vince for a couple of minutes, her hips gliding back and forth on him as his meaty rod slid in and out of her pussy. Nick could see her juices already on Vince's cock as she continued to bounce up and down on him, her cries filling the room as she clutched his shoulders. Nick had to admit, they were two of the largest cocks he had ever seen. There was no way his tiny dick could compare and satisfy his wife the way they were.

Mark moved up behind Missy, almost blocking Nick's view of his wife being fucked. The tall, black man spread Missy's ass cheeks as he aimed his cock at her dark star, and Nick felt his cock get even harder at the thought that these two giant men were going to spear his wife in both of her holes at the same time.

Missy glanced over her shoulder as Mark eased closer, the head of his cock pressing into her ass. "Oh god, Mark. I don't think I can," she said. "You're so big. Both of you. I can't…" Then Mark shoved his cock into her, and Missy cried out, clutching Vince tighter as he held her still.

"I wasn't asking you, slut," Mark growled as he shoved his cock into her, his hands gripping her hips tighter as he rammed into her.

Missy cried out, but Nick noticed she shoved herself backward to meet Mark's thrust. "Yes! Oh god!"

Mark thrust into her, ramming his cock in and out of her ass, driving her onto Vince's massive shaft as he did. Missy floundered under the assault, her head rolling side-to-side as she took every inch of her lover's cock.

Nick was amazed at the sight. His wife was stuffed with two massive cocks, her pale body pinned between two hulking black men as they used her to satisfy themselves, forcing her to take their cocks wherever they wanted to stick them, She hit the couch with a tight fist once and then Mark pounded into her even harder, his fingers digging into her as his hips slapped her ass, his cock spearing her pussy and spreading it wider than Nick could ever hope to do.

Vince continued to suck and pinch Missy's nipples as she thrashed between them, her body uncontrollable as they fucked her, creating a rhythm between them that kept her squirming. As Mark slid out of her pussy, Vince would thrust upward, driving into her even harder. Missy just braced herself between them and took each thrust of their cocks. Nick could see her body start to shudder as she cried out. "I'm coming!" Her whole body shook as the men held her, her flesh one tight knot as her orgasm ripped through her like a tornado. She kept calling out, begging them to keep fucking her, not to stop. When her orgasm finally subsided, she just collapsed between them, her head on Vince's shoulders.

Vince gripped her waist with his massive hands and then thrust up into her one more time, Nick knowing the man was emptying his seed into Missy, filling her married cunt with his love juice. Mark grunted, his fingers digging into her waist as he thrust into Missy one more time, pinning her against him as he emptied his cock into her eager ass. The sight was enough to send Nick over the edge, ropes of his own cum spewing out of his cock to cover his stomach and hand. He grunted as his cum covered him, but he couldn't take his eyes off his wife.

Mark smacked Missy's ass once, the slap leaving a large handprint on her pale skin as he slid his long cock out of her ass, cum dribbling out of her dark hole to fall between her legs. Vince shifted her off of him, sliding her over to the couch. Nick watched as his wife's dripping cunt slid off the length of Vince's manhood, their juices coating his rod with a bright sheen.

Missy looked over at her husband, grinning. "You know what to do," she said.

"Yeah, Cuck," Mark said as he sat beside Missy, one hand over her shoulders as his hand draped down and played with her nipple. "If you don't want Vince's baby, you better get over here and do your job."

Nick just nodded as he dropped to his knees and crawled over to where Missy sat between her lovers. Both men watched him as he positioned himself between his wife's thighs as she spread her legs for him. He could see the pearly drops of the men's cum dripping from her pussy and ass, coating her thighs as she opened herself up to her husband. Her pussy was swollen, her ass slightly open from Mark's cock, as Nick leaned in and ran his tongue over her slimy slit, tasting the mixture of her cum and the salty tang of Vince's seed. Nick buried his head there, lapping up the wetness, shoving his tongue in and out of his wife, making sure to get every dollop of cum from her cunt and ass.

The men had stopped watching him, turning their attention back to Missy. Vince was making out with her, his tongue twirling inside of her mouth, while Mark sucked on her breasts, his hand cupping her round globe while his tongue flicked over her nipple. Missy groaned as they ravished her body, squeezing her pussy and shoving cum into her husband's mouth.

When Nick thought he had swallowed every drop he could find, he sat back on his heels and just stared at the three on the couch. Vince broke the kiss and reached over, tweaking Missy's other nipple as Mark settled back on the couch. Missy reached out and stroked their still-hard cocks. "Boy, am I glad your dates went frigid tonight," she said. "This was definitely a great way to bring the night to an end."

Mark chuckled. "Oh, it isn't ending yet."

"Oh yeah," Vince said, grinning. "This booty call is still going."

Nick watched as his wife grinned, still stroking the men's cocks. "Now, that's what I like to hear. Men with stamina. Well, then, drink up, boys. We have a long night of sex ahead of us." She glanced down at Nick, cum still sticking to his face and stomach. "I'd clean up, Nick. I'm sure you're going to be needed again in a little while."

Nick moaned at the thought, but stood and turned toward the bathroom to wash his own cum and that of his wife's lovers off his face and body. The last thing he saw was Vince pulling Missy back down onto his cock and her mouth opening wide to accept it. Nick felt his dick start to stir to life again and rushed to clean up. He didn't want to miss too much of the action.

HOUSEWIFE'S REVENGE

Mike walked into the house, lost in thoughts of reports and files back at work that needed finished and looking forward to a nice calm evening at home. However, he hadn't stepped two feet into his house when those hopes shattered into a million confusing pieces. His wife, Sandy, sat in his recliner, or rather, she sat in the lap of the biggest black man Mike had ever seen in his recliner, the man's large hand on Sandy's bare thigh as if he owned her. The man, thick with muscles and dressed only in a pair of dark blue boxers sat there, holding Sandy, dressed only in a flimsy teddy, her nipples quite visible through the sheer fabric. Neither of them moved when Mike walked in, not concerned at all, it seemed, that they were caught doing whatever it was they were doing. Mike just stared, dumbfounded, not sure what to do or think. After several agonizing seconds of awkward silence, he mustered the courage to ask, "What the hell is going on, Sandy? Who is this, and why are you on his lap dressed like that?"

Sandy just smiled at him as she placed a hand on the black man's powerful chest. "Is there a particular order you would like those questions answered, or should I just answer them in whichever order I prefer?" When Mike just stood there, staring, Sandy shrugged and continued to speak. "Fine. I'll answer them in my own order then. First, this is Mark. He's here to help you out."

"Help me out?" Mike said, his tone belligerent. "Seems like he's here to help you out."

"Now, now," Sandy scolded him. "You had your chance to pick the order the answers came in and refused, so now you just stand there like a good little boy and listen." She took a deep breath as she slid an arm around Mark's thick shoulders, her fingers gliding back and forth over the man's dark skin. "Oh well, the answer actually solves three of your questions, so why not answer it now? As for why he's here, what's going on, and why am I in his lap, it's all because of you and your perverted computer activities." She cocked an eyebrow at him as if daring him to deny knowing what she meant.

However, Mike knew he couldn't do that, knew that if she had seen what was on his laptop, she knew he had been stalking the porn sites looking for cuckold videos and stories. He felt the heat of his embarrassment on his neck and cheeks as he stood there before his wife and her...lover? Mike's eyes popped wide as he realized what Mark must have been there for and what Sandy intended. "Sandy, those were just stories," Mike said, his words coming out in a rush as panic gripped him. "They weren't meant to be taken as reality. It was just a site I stumbled upon."

Sandy turned to Mark, running a finger along the man's strong chin and over his lips. "I don't believe you," she said. "Those stories were pretty intense, and I could tell you had watched several videos repeatedly. I bet you sat there jacking that little cock of yours off while you watched them, didn't you?" She turned to face him, her eyes narrowed into angry slits. "Didn't you, Mike? Didn't you sit there and watch another man being humiliated while his petite white wife took a black man's massive cock into her married pussy? Isn't that what got your tiny dick off?"

Mike squirmed where he stood, the words frozen in his mouth as he stared at his practically-naked wife sitting there, stroking another man's body. He didn't want to admit to his wife that she was right, that those videos had made him shoot his cum harder than just basic sex ever had.

Sandy grinned at him again. "Your silence is all the answer I need," she said. "So, here is what we're going to do. You're going to sit there like a good little cuckold and watch as Mark pounds your wife with his massive cock. You can even take that puny stick of yours out and stroke it while you watch me finally get satisfied. But, watch you will, because we both know that's what you truly want."

Mark shifted under Sandy, and Mike could see the man's giant bulge in the front of his boxers. "Are you going to talk him to death or are we going to do some fucking?" the man asked. "I want to get my dick wet with your married pussy, not listen to you two banter back and forth."

Sandy turned to him, kissing his cheek as she held his other with her small white hand. "Now, now, Mark, be patient," she cooed into his ear. "I had to let Mike know how you were going to be helping him, didn't I? He knows now, so we can get to our fun." She slid down to her knees in front of Mark, her gaze on her husband, though. "Are you ready, Mike?" she asked. "Are you ready to be a cuckold just like those men in the videos?"

Mike could only stand there and watch as his wife slid off the other man's lap, dropping to her knees in front of him as she turned her back on her husband. Her hands went to Mark's boxers, slipping her fingers into the waistband and sliding them down and off his powerful legs. Mike sucked in a breath when the other man's meaty rod sprang into sight. The thing was huge, at least ten inches long and four inches wide. Mike's own cock was nowhere near that size. He didn't know how his wife would even be able to take it.

Mark stared at the top of Sandy's blond head, her ample breasts swaying in the softness of her lingerie as she slid closer to his dark python. She reached out, gripping the huge shaft with her dainty hand, her fingers not even closing around his girth as she stroked him up and down, pre-cum bubbling up to the tip of his cock. Mark grinned over at Mike. "You might want to take a seat, Cuck," he said. "I'm going to take my time with your slut wife."

Mike stood still for a second, torn between wanting to tell the man in the recliner to get the hell out of his house and wanting to keep his gaze on his wife surrendering to the other man's delights. Finally, he gave in to what his mind craved and walked over to the couch and sat down, his gaze never leaving the others.

Sandy leaned forward, gliding her tongue over the top of Mark's velvet head, the strand of pre-cum stretching as she lifted her mouth a little. She then sucked it into her mouth, running her tongue over her lips as she did, a grin covering her face.

Mike groaned as he felt his cock stiffen in his pants. Reaching down, he stroked his cock, feeling it grow, but knowing it was nowhere near the size of Mark's.

Sandy swallowed the other man's dark rod, her small head dropping down onto it as far as she could go. Mike could imagine her tongue twirling around the man's thick manhood, the way his ridges and veins felt in her mouth as she sucked him off. Her body seemed so small as she knelt in front of him, one hand on Mark's thigh as with her other she massaged his balls.

Mark looked over at Mike and sneered. "Your wife gives good head, Cuck," he said. "Why don't you take that tiny dick of yours out so I can see why she wasn't getting satisfied?"

Mike did as Mark ordered, embarrassed to be stripping in front of the other man, but grateful to have his cock out where he could stroke it. He could feel his own excitement building within him as he watched his wife suck off that massive shaft. As soon as he was out of his pants and underwear, he sat back down on the couch, his four-inch dick as hard as it had ever been.

Mark laughed at him, his hand still gripping Sandy's head as he fucked her face. "You tried to fuck her with that?" he taunted. "Could you even get it past her entrance?" He shoved Sandy's head down harder on his cock. "Now, I know why she called me. Slut needs a real fucking with a real cock, not some toy."

Mike groaned at the man's words, but knew they were the truth. Sandy would never want his dick after Mark fucked her with his giant rod. How could she? Nothing Mike could do would ever satisfy her once Mark pounded her with his huge manhood.

Mark grabbed Sandy by the hair and pulled her up off her knees to her feet. With both hands he gripped her teddy and ripped it into shreds, the remnants hanging off her like tattered curtains. Sandy cried out and then giggled as Mark shoved the material off her shoulders to fall onto the floor at their feet. Mike watched as the other man reached up and took Sandy's swollen nipples in his fingers, twisting them until she screamed, her feet dancing in her pain. He pulled Sandy's mounds toward his mouth, reaching out with his tongue and flicking her hardened bud back and forth as with his other hand he roughly squeezed her other breast, mauling it in his fingers. Sandy pleaded for more as she ran her hands through his hair, gripping his head and holding it to her melons. Mike could see the pleasure on her face, see her ass wiggling just above the other man's rock-hard cock.

Mark then let go of her tit with his hand and shoved two fingers into her drenched pussy. As he nibbled on her nipple, he thrust his fingers in and out of her, her juices making a loud slurping noise as he finger-fucked her.

Sandy bounced up and down on his hand, humping the man's fingers as he sucked and bit on her nipple, pleading with him to do it harder. Mike wasn't sure if she meant the fingering or the biting, and Mark may not have known either, because he did both. Sandy screamed as Mark bit her sensitive bud harder, driving his fingers into her with such force, Mike could hear the man's knuckles pounding her folds from where he sat on the couch.

Mark didn't let up, however. As soon as he tired of fingering her, he pinched her nipples again, using them to turn her around, so that she faced her husband. Mark bent her forward so that her huge breasts dangled and then shoved his fingers back into her cunt.

Sandy stared at her husband, her face contorted with her lust as she bounced back onto Mark's thick fingers. "Yes!" she cried out. "Oh god, yes! Even his fingers are bigger than your cock."

Mike just stared at his wife's huge tits, her nipples hard pebbles due to the other man's attention.

Mark ran his hand up her back and into her hair, taking a fistful and jerking her head back, stretching her throat as he forced her to look upward. "This is how you treat a slut," he growled at Mike. "Your wife is a good one, too, Cuck. I can't wait to sink my thick black cock into her married pussy." He jerked his fingers out of her cunt and pulled her back so she could clean her juices from them.

Sandy swallowed his fingers, her tongue twirling around each one as she groaned. Mike groaned as well, wishing he was the one cleaning those fingers, tasting his wife.

Satisfied, Mark released her head and then slapped her ass. "You ready to get what you begged me for the other day?" he asked.

Mike felt his brows pinch in confusion. *They had this planned for days? My wife actually reached out to this man and begged him to fuck her in front of her husband? When? When did she do this?*

"God, yes," Sandy groaned. "I need it, need a real man's cock." She grinned at Mike, and he watched as Mark gripped her waist, his dark skin a sharp contrast to her pale flesh. Sandy reached back between her legs, taking Mark's massive cock in her hand and guiding it toward her drenched pussy. "Are you ready, Mike?" she asked him. "Are you ready to be a cuckold? Are you ready for another man to stretch your wife's cunt like you never could? Say it. Tell me you want it, you little pervert."

Mike swallowed the humiliation, but couldn't deny that even though his stomach was twisting in jealous knots, he did indeed want it, wanted her to give herself to Mark, to take his thicker, wider cock into her married pussy. He found himself nodding as he said, "Yes. Please. Oh god, fuck him, Sandy."

She bit her lower lips as she guided Mark's manhood to her wetness, sliding it back and forth on her slit first, teasing herself before she popped the head into her entrance and speared herself with the man's meaty rod. She gasped, a purring noise escaping her lips as her cunt swallowed the man's cock. "God, he's so big, Mike," she said. "So much bigger than your pathetic cock." She gripped Mark's thighs, bouncing her ass up and down on the man as she fucked him, his hands still gripping her hips as he watched her plump ass rising and falling on his slick shaft.

Mike could see his wife's juices slipping from her pussy, see her wetness coating the man's dark shaft as her pussy lifted up and down on it, covering his cock and dripping onto his balls. He then started stroking his own cock, gripping it with only two fingers, which was all he needed to hold it, and jerking himself off with vigor as he watched the pleasure on his wife's face.

Mark lifted her and then yanked her back down on his cock, fucking her from underneath as her massive tits bounced and jiggled. She kept whimpering as his cock stretched her, her legs wrapped around his thighs, spreading herself wide for him. She dropped her head, surrendering to the cock inside of her, the one that stretched her and filled her. Her breathing grew louder, mixing with her moans of pleasure as she bounced up and down on Mark's manhood. Then Mike saw her mouth pop open, her eyes go wide as she screamed, "I'm coming! Oh god, I'm coming!" Her whole body tightened as she threw her head back, her tits swaying as her body started to shake.

Mike could just sit there and watch, stroking his own cock as another man made his wife come, something he had never been able to do with his tiny dick.

As soon as her orgasm subsided, Mark shoved her off his shaft and onto the floor, twirling her over to her back with his foot. He stood above her, stroking his own throbbing cock for a few seconds before long ropes of cum spewed from the head of his cock to cover Sandy below him. White streams of Mark's seed landed across her face, her breasts, and along her stomach, coating her in globs of his spunk.

Mike just stared as the other man covered his wife in his jizz, marking her as his slut, his hand still vigorously jerking his cock off.

Sandy just laid there, giggling as she opened her mouth to catch stray droplets of cum. With her hands, she smeared the white goo all over her body, coating her tits with Mark's passion.

Mark glanced up at Mike, a smirk on his face, and then before he could stop it, Mike came all over his hand and stomach, ropes of his sticky mess exploding from his tiny dick.

Mark just stood there and laughed at the man before walking over to Sandy, reaching down and grabbing her by the hair, lifting her to his cock. "Clean it, slut," he growled.

Sandy knelt in front of him, a drop of his cum dripping from her nipple as she swallowed his still-hard shaft, running her tongue over the tip to get any leftover remnants of his seed. She licked up and down his cock, her tongue slurping up their juices. With his manhood clean, she lowered her head to his balls, sucking each one dry of their sex before falling back to sit on her heels.

Mark just grinned at her. "Now, that was worth taking time for," he said. "Make sure you call me when you're ready for some more of my dark meat." He then got dressed and left, Sandy still kneeling on the floor and Mike sitting on the couch, his hand still holding his shrinking dick, cum dripping from his knuckles.

Sandy stood and walked over to her husband. "Now, that was a real cock," she purred. She then gripped Mike by the hair and pulled his face to her breast. "Now, suck his cum from my body, Cuck, and then, I'll tell you how the rest of your life is going to go."

Mike groaned as the other man's salty seed filled his nostrils. Without hesitation, he ran his tongue over his wife's massive mounds, lapping up the other man's cum from his wife's body. He sucked her nipples dry and then ran his tongue down her stomach to make sure there was no cum left on her belly. When he finished there, she made him stand and kiss each drop of Mark's cum from her face. As a final show of his humiliation,

Sandy grabbed his hand and lifted it to his lips, making him suck his own cum into his mouth.

Mike did everything she asked, his cock becoming hard again with the shame of being turned into a cuckold.

When he finished, she made him kneel on the floor as she sat on the couch, propping her feet in his lap. "Now, Cuckold, since that is what you are, let me tell you how life is going to go from this day forward, and all the cocks I'm going to fuck."

Mike took a deep breath as he sat there, his life now exactly what he had fantasized. He was a cuckold to a hotwife.

CUCKOLDED BY THE NEIGHBORS

CHAPTER ONE

"It'll be fun," Jenny said as she started putting together a small bag of goodies to take over to their neighbors. "Mark and Brenda have been trying to get us to come hang out with them for weeks, and it's the perfect day for it. Mark's even offered to grill while we lay out and enjoy the pool. They even have a full bar to help us relax. What's there not to like?"

Brian groaned inwardly. There was plenty not to like in his mind, the first of which was how he had noticed his wife staring at Mark's broader shoulders and more powerful frame. He hadn't missed how the two of them had smiled back and forth at each other when talking or how Jenny always seemed to stand so close to Mark whenever they were around each other, touching him when she giggled at one of his jokes. She never giggled at Brian's jokes. That Jenny was infatuated with their neighbor was quite obvious, and Mark didn't hide the fact that he welcomed her attention, not even when his own wife was around. "And now you're going to wear that skimpy bathing suit over there for him to ogle your body," Brian continued his whining. "I just think it's a little too much friendliness between neighbors."

Jenny rolled her eyes as she turned around to face him, the fabric of her bathing suit top barely covering her ample breasts, her nipples already straining against the flimsy material. "You really do have too much imagination," she said. "Of course, I think he's good looking—damn good looking, actually—but that doesn't mean I'd ever do anything without your permission." She gave him a wink before turning back around to finish loading the bag.

He stopped what he was doing and stared at her slender back, soaking in her scantily clad ass that he just knew Mark was going to be trying to grab all afternoon. "Without my permission?" He couldn't believe what he heard. Was she actually thinking of having sex with their neighbor? "Don't you think that just proves my point about this being a bad idea?"

She shook her head, not turning around to face him. "No. All I think it proves is that you're a little paranoid. Now, be a good boy and go get your bathing suit on." She glanced over her shoulder at him and smirked with a bounce of her eyebrows.

"Good boy? You're enjoying this a little too much already." Still, he left the kitchen to carry out her orders, thinking this whole afternoon was a giant mistake and wishing he had the guts to call the entire thing off. His stomach was a mass of knots as he slipped out of his pants and moved to fetch his bathing suit, images of how Mark and Jenny touched each other when they talked floating through his head. Nothing overtly sexual, which was probably the problem. No, it was more casual caresses on the arm as she laughed at one of Mark's jokes or the lingering hug when they greeted each other, the friendly peck on the cheek a little too friendly.

As he slid his bathing suit up his legs, Brian had to tuck his hardening cock to the side to get it inside, his growing manhood contradicting his inward jealousy, which frustrated him even more. The idea of seeing his wife with another man had always turned him on, but not their neighbor, and not in reality. It was a fantasy, something for him to jerk off to when she had one of her constant headaches. Brian bet she'd never have a headache with Mark.

He touched his cock before pulling his bathing suit all the way up, stroking it to even fuller life as he thought of his wife down on her knees in front of another man, sucking his cock to life, her giant tits swaying as…

"Stop touching your dick, Brian, and get your ass out here so we can go," Jenny called from the kitchen, making Brian jump as if she had walked in on him and caught him masturbating. Jenny didn't know he jacked off to images of her with others, didn't know he jacked off period.

Did she?

He finished putting on his bathing suit, slipped on a T-shirt, and headed out of the bedroom. When he reached the kitchen, Jenny stood there in her skimpy bikini, the bag of snacks in one hand and a beach towel in the other. He just stared at her a moment, his eyes wide as he soaked in her practically naked body. "Aren't you going to wear one of your cover-ups?"

Jenny laughed. "And why would I do that? I'm just going to be taking it off once I get there. I can't exactly go swimming or enjoy the sun if I'm wearing a cover-up."

"But what about the other neighbors?" he asked, still astonished that she would walk around outside with most of her body exposed, especially her ass and tits. "Are you planning on giving everyone a free show?"

She grinned as she walked past him, wiggling her ass as she did. "If you got it, flaunt it, right?" She winked at him as she passed him. "Now, let's go get into some trouble."

He groaned again as he watched her walk to the front door, sashaying her ass for dramatic effect. He really hoped old man Harrison wasn't in his front yard cutting grass right then.

CHAPTER TWO

Of course, Old Man Harrison *was* out in his front yard when they walked across their lawn, and he didn't hesitate to stop and stare at Jenny as she sashayed across their front lawn to the Bennetts. Brian just glared at the old man as he followed his wife.

Old Man Harrison just shrugged as if to say who could blame him for looking.

Brian continued to follow Jenny toward the Bennetts front door, still thinking this was a bad idea, but unable to call it off without appearing to be a total dick. When they reached the front door, Jenny stepped to the side and gestured for him to knock. He sighed, but did as she wanted, knocking twice on the hardwood door, hoping the Bennets forgot they had invited them over and were gone. He wasn't so lucky, however, and a few seconds after he knocked, Mark opened the door, his large dark frame intimidating to Brian but an aphrodisiac to Jenny as the man stood there in nothing but his bathing suit.

"Hey, neighbors," Mark said as he gestured for them to enter his home. "Glad you made it. Brenda and I have wanted to have the two of you over for quite some time."

Jenny flowed past Brian, smiling as she reached out and touched Mark's bare chest as she passed him. "I agree," she said. "We should have done this a long time ago."

Brian worried about knowing what *this* was in his wife's mind. "Hey, Mark," he said, trying his best to sound calm in the throes of his jealousy. "Thanks for having us over."

Mark patted Brian's back after he shut the door and started to guide them through the front of the house toward the kitchen. "My pleasure. What kind of neighbors would we be if we didn't share the good times?"

The kind who didn't stare at my wife, Brian thought as he followed the others through the house.

When they reached the kitchen, Brenda was putting the finishing touches on a pasta salad, standing by the kitchen counter in her bikini, which was just as skimpy as Jenny's if not more so. Brian tried hard not to stare, but found it difficult as Brenda's dark ass cheeks hung out both sides of her skimpy bottoms, the fabric practically swallowed by her ass crack, calling his eyes to stare. When she turned to greet them, her large breasts oozed over the sides of her top, which barely covered her hard nipples. She was gorgeous, a black goddess, and Brian wondered why Mark would flirt with Jenny when he had Brenda to come home to every night.

"Hey, neighbors," Brenda squealed as she left what she was doing to give Brian and Jenny both hugs, lingering on Jenny almost as long as Mark usually did. "I'm so glad you're here."

"God, Brenda, you look amazing," Jenny said as she held the other woman out at arms' length and gawked at her body. "I love that bathing suit."

"Oh, please," Brenda said, waving off the compliment. "To be honest, it took me forever to find it. Being just the two of us here, we hardly ever use bathing suits. The sun feels so good on my skin. I almost had to wear an old shorts outfit today until I found this thing in the back of one of my drawers."

"With that body, I'm sure you would have looked sexy in anything," Jenny said. "Of course, if you had told us skinny dipping was an option...." She giggled as she set the bag of snacks she brought on the kitchen table.

Mark laughed. "Skinny dipping is always an option."

Brian just smiled, forcing a small laugh past his lips. He didn't want to seem prudish, but his gut twisted at the thought of Mark being naked around Jenny. The man's cock was visible enough from the outline in his bathing suit, and from what Brian could see, Mark's manhood made his look like he hadn't reached puberty, yet.

"How about we get this party started?" Mark suggested. "I have a cooler of beer already out by the pool and a pitcher of margaritas just waiting to be guzzled. It's too beautiful of a day to miss standing around a boring old kitchen."

"Agreed," Brenda said as she picked up a vegetable tray from the counter and headed for the back door.

"I'm game," Jenny added as she started to follow Brenda out the sliding glass doors to the back patio.

Brian forced himself to smile as he nodded. "A beer sounds great." Maybe it would help cool down the jealousy he felt right then.

The Bennetts' backyard was an oasis from the real world with a grill and bar set off to the south of the pool, chaise lounge chairs along the decking, and even a concrete table with benches in the shallow end of the pool. A round table with chairs and an umbrella sat next to the grill, and that's where Brenda carried the tray of snacks while Mark went behind the bar to get everyone their drinks.

Jenny placed their towels on a lounge chair and sauntered up to the bar. "Wow," she said. "Your place looks amazing. I'm surprised we ever see you out front. I think I'd live back here."

Mark chuckled as he poured the ladies margaritas. "Your home should be a sanctuary from the world," he said. "Make it so that you'd rather be there than anywhere else is my motto."

Brian sat in one of the chairs around the table as Brenda uncovered the vegetable tray. "I'd say you've done an awesome job of that," he said. "As Jenny said, I'd live out here. And your privacy fence is high enough to give you complete isolation."

"Although, now that I know you both go without bathing suits, I may have to peek over the fence more often," Jenny said, grinning.

Mark glanced at her, his face a mask of lusty hunger. "Peek over anytime," he said. "See anything you like, then feel free to climb the fence and join." He winked at her, and Brian felt the knot in his stomach grow tighter.

CHAPTER THREE

"I'm ready for one of those margaritas," Brenda said as she moved over to the bar, standing real close to Jenny, Brian noticed. "This heat makes me extra thirsty."

Jenny leaned on the bar, her tits almost falling out of her bathing suit as she watched Mark fix their drinks. It was quite obvious Mark noticed. The funny part to Brian was that Brenda seemed to notice as well and didn't seem at all upset by Jenny's display or her husband's frank approval. Brian expected their neighbor to be jealous over his wife's obvious attention to Mark, but Brenda seemed to take it all in stride as if nothing unusual was happening in front of her.

With drinks in hand, they all ventured over to the pool, sliding down into the sun-warm water one step at a time. Brian noticed Jenny moved to lean against the wall, and that Mark moved closer to her while Brenda moved to the other side of

Brian, leaving Brian and Mark standing beside each other. At first, he thought it odd, that the women would flank the men, and that the men weren't standing beside their own wives. Still, it was a small get-together and a very large pool. He would force his insecurities down and focus on relaxing and having fun. He would. At least, he thought he would until he noticed Jenny staring at Mark's crotch, a smile curving the corners of her lips upward.

Glancing in the same direction, Brian couldn't help but stare as well. With Mark's bathing suit now wet, the material hugged the man's cock—his massive cock. The thing had to be at least ten inches long and more than three inches thick. How in the hell could anyone take a monster like that into their cunts?

"Isn't it something, Jenny?" Brenda asked as she slid closer to Brian, her eyes watching Jenny gawk at how big Mark's manhood was even limp.

Jenny glanced away, her cheeks turning red, embarrassed from being so blatantly caught, Brian assumed. "I'm sorry," she stammered, moving a little away from Mark. Brian also noticed she didn't move *that* far away from Mark. "I've just never seen a cock that big before. Brian's is so small compared to Mark's. I shouldn't have been staring, though."

"Jenny!" Brian shouted, more so because of the embarrassment of being called small in front of their neighbors than her open admission of staring at Mark's shaft.

"Oh, don't be embarrassed, sweetie," Brenda said as she moved past Brian to get closer to Jenny. "Not many white women see a cock this big. You should take advantage of it while you can. Trust me, I don't mind. I get plenty of Mark's massive rod whenever I want him, and he sure loves pounding into a white woman's pussy. Says it always feels so tight because it's hardly ever been stretched like a pussy should."

Brian just stood and watched as Brenda practically gave Jenny permission to check out her husband's cock. *What the hell is going on here?*

"You really don't mind?" Jenny asked without ever taking her eyes off Mark's crotch. Brian could see the man's cock getting harder inside of his bathing suit from the attention Jenny was giving him, and she hadn't even touched him yet.

"By all means," Brenda said. "Brian's cock isn't even making a bump in his suit; I can only imagine how deprived for a real cock you've been. Mark can show you anything you want to see." Brenda slid over beside Brian again, but this time she was between him and her husband, her attention solely on Jenny and Mark, almost blocking Brian from watching. "Don't by shy, sweetie. Explore that monster."

Brian was about to say something, say how his wife wouldn't do it, wouldn't touch another man's cock, but stopped, his mouth open, as Jenny slid through the water to get closer to Mark. Brian watched as his petite wife reached out and took the strings to Mark's bathing suit in her hands, pulling them loose. She didn't even look into Mark's face, but rather kept staring at the cock she was about to reveal. Inwardly, Brian begged his wife to stop before she went too far, but Jenny showed no intention of stopping. He watched as under the surface of the water, Jenny pulled Mark's bathing suit wide open, the man's hard cock popping into sight. Jenny released the bathing suit, wrapping her hand around Mark's manhood and stroking it, her mouth slightly open, her tongue appearing along her bottom lip.

"That's right, honey," Brenda said. "Feel what a real cock feels like. That's what a woman needs fucked with, not some tiny little nub of a cock that just leaves us wanting more." Brenda turned and glanced at Brian, a smirk across her face. "She may never touch your little dick again once she has a taste of a real man."

Brian opened his mouth to say something, but his words were cut off by his wife's mesmerized words. "I want it in my mouth." Her gaze fixated on the massive rod in her hands. "Can I? Please?"

Mark moved over to the side of the pool, sliding up as his bathing suit floated down his legs and off as he walked. Naked, he sat on the edge of the pool, his legs dangling in the water as his cock stood tall and proud. Brian could only watch as Jenny slid through the water toward their neighbor's cock, forgetting that Brian was even there, forgetting that she promised she wouldn't do anything without his permission. It was almost like Mark's cock hypnotized her, calling her to it.

Mark had yet to say anything, just stood there—now sat there—and allowed Jenny to grope him while his wife watched. Now, Mark just glanced down at Jenny, his lips curved up in a grin of invitation.

Jenny gripped Mark's cock again as she stood between his legs, his cock even with her breasts before she leaned down and ran her tongue over the head of his cock. Brian almost groaned out loud as he watched his wife swallow their neighbor's massive cock, her hand running up and down his hardness as she sucked him off. Mark looked over Jenny's head at Brian, another smirk on his lips, but this one for a whole other reason. Brian just felt the knot in his stomach twist again as his cock twitched to life.

CHAPTER FOUR

Brian watched as Jenny's head bobbed up and down, Mark's hand on her head, guiding her as he watched her enjoy his thick cock.

"Look at how your wife is devouring Mark's cock," Brenda said as she leaned up against Brian. He felt her hand slide down his stomach to his cock, rubbing his hard member through his bathing suit. "You want to tell me you hate it, but your body doesn't lie, and from what I'm feeling, she'll love having my husband's long, thick, black cock buried inside of her. We'll have to find another use for you, won't we?" She gripped his cock, squeezing it hard. "Get out of your bathing suit and get your little ass up by those chairs." She then turned and moved to the stairs as she untied her bathing suit top, letting it fall to the pool's surface as she walked.

Brian could only stare as her dark, ample breasts came into full view, her hard nipples tiny buds in the middle of her dark aureoles. He glanced back over his shoulder and watched as Mark slid down into the water, pushing Jenny against the wall, her tits sliding along the tile as he pulled her ass out a little. Mark stepped behind Jenny, his hands on her waist as his cock slid up and down her ass crack.

"Come here, my little boy," Brenda said as she stretched an arm out, her fingers wiggling for him to come to her. She had already stripped out of her bikini bottoms, her legs open so that Brian had a great view of her bald pussy. "Come sit beside me and watch as your wife gets fucked for the first time. She'll feel like a virgin compared to what she's used to being fucked with."

Brian obeyed without question, sitting down on the chair beside Brenda as he turned his gaze to his wife. Mark had his hands on Jenny's hips as he growled into her ears. "Are you ready for a real man? Do you want this cock?"

"Please!" Jenny screamed as she looked back at Mark over her shoulder. "Fuck me. I want your cock. Give it to me!"

Brian felt the twist in his stomach as he watched his wife beg for another man's cock, a much larger cock. He felt Brenda's hand toying with his cock, stroking it as they watched Mark drive his monster into Jenny. She only used two fingers to stroke him, and Jenny had to use her entire hand to grip Mark's cock, and her fingers hadn't even closed around his shaft.

Jenny pushed her ass back as she continued to beg Mark to take her, no longer caring that she begged for another man's cock in front of her husband. Mark gripped her hips tighter as he thrust his cock all the way inside of her cunt, making her gasp as she clawed at the side of the pool. "God, yes!" Jenny screamed. "So fucking big; your cock is so fucking big. God, you're splitting me open."

Brian felt his stomach churn at her words. She had never screamed out like this when he fucked her. Would she ever want his cock again?

"See?" Brenda asked him. "That's how a woman reacts when a real man fucks her. Now, get your little white ass down between my legs and start licking my pussy. The only thing we need you for now is your mouth. Your cock is useless."

Brian scampered off the chair, kneeling at the end as he leaned over the bottom of the chair, burying his face between Brenda's dark legs as she shoved his face down toward her pussy, which glistened with her wetness. As he slid his tongue up between her folds, he heard his wife screaming out, begging for Mark to fuck her harder. Brenda put her hands on his head, holding his mouth to her pussy as she slid her cunt up and down on his mouth, grinding against him.

"That's it, boy, hear your wife begging for my husband's cock," Brenda taunted him, her thighs clamped around his head as she held his face to her pussy. "She'll never want that tiny dick of yours again after having a real cock in her pussy. Oh, but don't you worry. There will be plenty for your mouth to do. You do have a talented tongue." She ground her cunt up and down on his face to the point Brian thought he would suffocate. "Keep licking!" she snapped. "Don't you dare stop licking my pussy, boy, or I'll spank your ass good and hard in front of your wife. You're my little bitch now, and I'll use you as often as I need. Your cute little wife will be busy serving my husband's cock. She's a real black cock whore now."

Brian felt his cock twitch at everything Brenda said to him as he lapped at her pussy and the shame of it burned his cheeks. Still, he couldn't deny how turned on it made him to know that Jenny would be Mark's toy while he served Brenda. His life, especially his sex life, would never be the same now that his wife had felt a real cock between her legs.

Brenda cried out as she clamped her thighs around his head even harder, her legs shaking as she pressed his mouth even tighter onto her pussy, her orgasm flooding through her. Brian continued to lick at her pussy as he held her thighs, his tongue gliding over her swollen clit as she held his head in place. It didn't take long before her climax subsided, and she released his head, smiling down at him. "Yes, we will definitely make good use of that tongue of yours," she said as she ran her tongue over her lips. "Now, get your ass up here. I want to see you stroke that little dick of yours while my husband finishes claiming your wife."

Brian didn't say anything, happy to at least be offered some form of release. Quickly, he scampered up until he sat on the edge of Brenda's chair, his ass half hanging off as she wrapped an arm around him. She touched his hard cock, giggling. "Such a sad excuse for a dick."

Brian only nodded, knowing she was right.

CHAPTER FIVE

As soon as Brian balanced himself beside Brenda on her chair, she gave him permission to stroke his pitiful excuse for a dick. He needed no further urging, his cock throbbing from what Brenda forced him to endure and the sounds of his wife being fucked coming from the pool. As his gaze landed on his wife and Mark, the giant black man having her bent over on the pool steps as he stood behind her and pounded into her, Brian couldn't help but notice how thick Mark's cock was. Brian barely needed two fingers to jack himself off, and it would take Jenny's entire hand on Mark's cock, and Brian doubted she would be able to close her fingers. Jenny's face was a mask of pure pleasure as Mark dug his fingers into her hips and shoved his monster shaft in and out of her wet cunt. At one point, Jenny opened her eyes, looking at Brian, but he doubted she even saw him, lost in Mark's cock as she was.

"God, Mark, you're so fucking big," she groaned. "I've never been so full."

Brian felt the twisting in his stomach as his cock throbbed even more, hating what he heard, but unable to deny how it made his cock hard.

"Oh, god," Jenny shrieked. "Mark, don't stop. Oh, god, I'm...I'm...Oh, god, I'm coming!" Brian watched as his petite wife shoved herself back onto mark's giant spear, impaling her pussy onto him as her body shook with the strongest orgasm he had ever witnessed her having, and it wasn't him who gave it to her. He doubted he would ever be able to make her come after this. She wouldn't want his miserable little dick as Brenda said.

As Jenny's body shook, Brian heard Mark grunt as he pulled her back, holding her in place on his cock, and Brian knew the man was coming inside of Jenny without protection of any kind. Jenny didn't even seem to care as she rode the wave of her climax, Mark keeping her from slipping from the pool steps. When their orgasms subsided, Mark spun Jenny around to face him, his powerful hands going to her back as he pressed the smaller woman against him and kissed her hard. Jenny just hung on him as she surrendered to the kiss.

When they broke the kiss, Jenny looked over at Brian, and the way she stared at him, stroking his dick with two fingers, was all it took to cause him to shoot his load all over his chest. He grunted and then Brenda laughed at him. "Is that all you had?

Two small strands of cum? I bet there's a gallon inside your pretty wife there. No wonder she eagerly took every drop."

Brian felt his face flush with shame as he stared at Jenny who only joined in the laughter.

"Now, you clean that shit up so we can get back to the cooking," Brenda ordered.

Brian moved to obey her, but she stopped him with a shake of her head. "You're not wasting a towel on such a little amount. Lick it up. Right now."

Brian felt his cheeks burn hotter, but he dared not refuse the woman. As he tried not to watch Jenny, he lifted his hand to his mouth and sucked his own cum from his fingers. He then swiped the white gunk from his chest and stomach and swallowed it as well.

"Well, I never would have believed it," Jenny said. "He's a little cum eater. This will be fun."

Brian finally looked up and saw Jenny and Mark walking toward them, water dripping from their naked bodies as Mark had his arm around Jenny's waist, keeping her pressed to him as they walked, claiming her in front of her husband. Brian knew there was nothing he could do about it. Jenny had found the cock she craved, and he would just have to deal with it, enduring the humiliation that she preferred another man to her own husband.

"Oh, believe it, sweetie," Brenda said as she pushed Brian off her chair and rose to her feet. "You'll discover this husband of yours has other uses besides disappointing you with that tiny dick of his. I'll be more than happy to show you while Mark gives you a good pounding. I know you don't want to give up his cock after you felt it in your tight pussy."

"Oh, I don't think I could," Jenny said as she glanced down at Mark's flaccid member, which still looked three times bigger than Brian's hard cock. She then turned to Brenda. "As long as you don't mind sharing, that is."

"Oh, I'll have your hubby here keeping me satisfied," Brenda said. "I have plenty of uses for a white man with a tiny dick." She patted Brian's chest. "We'll have plenty of fun, won't we?"

Brian just nodded his head, a lump in his throat keeping him from saying anything. He watched as Mark slid his hand into Jenny's, their fingers intertwined as they walked over to the grill. Brenda swatted Brian's ass, ordering him to fix them all drinks. "Yes, ma'am," he said, weakly, knowing his role in all their lives had just changed, and his cock throbbed at the thought.

CUCKOLDED BY HER EX

CHAPTER ONE

Tommy watched as Chrissy slid into her tight red dress, the fabric hugging her voluptuous hips and cupping her ample breasts as she straightened the dress into place. When she turned to face him, her blond hair framing her face, he couldn't help but notice how her cleavage oozed over the low-cut neckline, begging people to stare at her large bosom, wishing they could have the treasures she hid, treasures Tommy knew wouldn't stay hidden for long. "Are you sure you want to do this?" he asked his wife. "It's not too late to change your mind."

She turned to him, grinning. "And why on earth would I want to change my mind? I haven't seen Jack in five years. It'll be nice to see if things still click in certain areas." She bounced her eyebrows at Tommy.

Tommy groaned inwardly, knowing exactly what his wife wanted to have click. With a deep breath, he continued his whining. "But, don't you think it's dangerous going out with your ex-husband? I mean, there's a reason he's your ex and not your current husband." From everything Tommy had heard about her previous marriage, Chrissy and Jack fought constantly about any silly thing they could. The only time, apparently, that they weren't arguing is when they were fucking each other's brains out. Sex was the only thing the two of them clicked over.

Chrissy nodded as she walked over to where Tommy stood, his arms hanging limp at his sides as he watched her approach. "Oh, there is, trust me. He was a total ass who cheated on me every chance he could, but then, I'm not meeting him in order to date him again." She leaned closer to Tommy, taking her hand and rubbing his small cock through his slacks, knowing he wore a pair of dull-pink panties she always made him wear whenever she went out on one of her dates. "You know why I'm meeting him, don't you, my little sissy?"

Tommy swallowed the lump in his throat. "Yes," he whispered, his cock twitching slightly at her pet name for him.

"Tell me," she ordered him, her voice still a soft whisper as she urged him to humiliate himself with her goals for the night. "Tell me why I'm meeting my ex-husband and not staying home with you, instead." She leaned even closer, her lips brushing against his ear as she whispered again, "Tell me."

Her breath on the side of his face, her voice in his ear, and her hand on his growing cock sent tremors through his body. He closed his eyes as he said, "You're going because you miss how he used to fuck you. You want his cock."

She ran her tongue over his ear. "And tell me why I want his cock."

"Because it's bigger than mine," he forced himself to admit, his eyes still closed as his cock grew to its full four inches in her hand. "And thicker. Because he fucks you better than I can." The admission turned his cheeks and neck red with the shame, but he knew it was true. Chrissy never ceased to remind him how Jack could make her come over and over, and how she missed the way he would assault her cunt.

She kissed the side of Tommy's face. "That's right. He can fuck me much better than you, and you want me to be satisfied, right? You like when I come home all stretched out, right? Tell me you want it. Ask me to go fuck Jack."

Tommy groaned as he stood there, but he knew he would do as she ordered. He always did as she ordered. "Please, Chrissy, fuck Jack. Let him please you where I can't." He swallowed again. "Please."

Chrissy backed away, patting his chest as she did. "Now, that's a good boy. You know you love when I bring you a nice creampie to clean up. And I promise, tonight, you'll have plenty to lap up."

He nodded, his cock twitching even though his stomach twisted into a tight wad of knots. He hated how his body betrayed him. He didn't want his wife fucking her ex-husband, but his body called him a liar as his cock strained against the panties she made him wear under his pants.

"Now, you stay here and enjoy your night while I go out dancing," she said, her hand still on his chest, her smile promising things he was afraid to have delivered. "Jack and I will be back for the main event. Make sure the house is tidy and the bed made. When we come in, you will make sure we each have drinks, and then, you will make yourself fade into the shadows. You may watch, but no touching, not even your little cock. Is that understood?" She gave him a serious look, and Tommy knew better than to disobey her.

"Yes, ma'am," he said. "I understand."

"Good," she said. "Now, wish me a good time and perhaps I'll send you a couple of pictures to keep your fantasies going."

The knot in his stomach twisted. He knew he was in for a miserable couple of hours as she went out with her ex, leaving Tommy alone there with his imagination. "Please have a good time, Chrissy. I hope you enjoy your time with Jack."

She grinned at him. "Oh, I'm sure I will." She kissed him on the cheek, rubbed his cock one more time, and then grabbed her purse and left.

Tommy just stared at the door a moment, his stomach churning, and his cock throbbing.

CHAPTER TWO

Tommy made sure to do everything Chrissy had commanded of him. He made the bed, fluffing the pillows the way Chrissy liked them and then made sure the living room and bathroom were clean. He took his time, knowing that Chrissy would be at least two hours, and with nothing else to do, his mind would go bonkers with him just sitting around imagining what Jack was doing to his wife. Or what she was doing to him.

Tommy should have known when Jack came back around a week ago that things would turn sexual quickly. Chrissy never hid the fact that she missed Jack's monster cock between her legs and how much of a disappointment Tommy's tiny dick was in comparison. Chrissy had even started making Tommy wear women's panties because, as she put it, he didn't really have a cock, but more of a giant clit. She would even make him jack off while wearing the panties so he would come inside the fabric. She would sit beside him as he stroked his cock, telling him how sad that even hard, his cock didn't poke out the top of the panties he wore. As soon as Jack reached back out, even knowing she was married again, Chrissy started talking about him while Tommy was lapping at her pussy, reciting Jack's prowess at taking her and pounding her like a real man would.

Tommy's phone dinged, pulling him out of his miserable reminiscing. He glanced over, expecting it to be a warning that Chrissy and her ex were on their way to the house, but he saw something else, instead. Chrissy had sent him a picture of Jack's hand on her bare breast, his fingers pinching her nipple. From what Tommy could tell, they were outside somewhere, probably near Jack's car.

Tommy felt his cock twitch as the knot in his stomach twisted tighter. He rubbed his hardness through his panties, knowing he wasn't allowed to jack off yet. He wouldn't get that privilege until after Chrissy had finished humiliating him in front of her ex, proving to Jack what a sissy of a man she had married after divorcing Jack.

Tommy was still staring at the picture when another one came in, this one of Chrissy sucking Jack's massive cock. Tommy could only stare at the long, thick shaft his wife swallowed, her lips stretched wide as she took as much into her tiny mouth as she could. Tommy rubbed his cock harder.

The next picture was of Chrissy bent over the trunk of Jack's car, her skirt pulled up around her waist and her panties down around her knees, legs spread as she glanced back at the camera over her shoulder. Tommy just groaned as he stared at his wife's pale ass cheeks fully exposed for another man, offering her married pussy to her ex, the man who had cheated on her.

Then a text came in. *We are heading that way now, my little sissy. Please make sure I have a glass of wine and that there is a whiskey neat for Jack. I hope you're ready to see your wife truly fucked like she deserves.*

Tommy sighed, knowing the real humiliation was about to begin. He typed back, *Yes, ma'am,* and then went to slip into his jeans and a T-shirt before fixing the drinks. He kept the panties on, knowing Chrissy would more than likely make him strip later on in the evening to embarrass him even more. She would not allow an opportunity such as that to pass.

He had just finished fixing the drinks and carried them into the living room when the front door opened and Chrissy stumbled in with the tall, muscular Jack right behind her. Chrissy twirled as soon as they were in the door, wrapping her arms around Jack's neck and kissing him soundly, her breasts pressed firmly against her ex's chest. Tommy stood there, watching and holding their drinks, as Jack slid his hands down Chrissy's back, cupping her ass as he pulled her skirt up with his fingers until the cups of her ass cheeks showed. Chrissy groaned as she pushed her round ass back into Jack's hands.

When the kiss was broken, Chrissy turned and smiled at Tommy. "Good boy," she said as she reached for her glass of wine on her way to the couch.

Jack smirked at Tommy as he walked over, taking the highball of whiskey and followed Chrissy to the couch. Tommy just stood where he was, waiting for instructions.

Chrissy sipped her wine as she draped one leg over Jack's legs, snuggling closer to him, her thighs parted a little, pulling her skirt up and revealing that she no longer wore her panties. She glanced over at Tommy, grinning as she stared at him. "We had such a good time tonight," she told him as she ran a hand through Jack's thick, dark hair.

"Oh, but baby, it's far from over, right?" Jack asked as he leaned in and nibbled Chrissy's ear, making her moan as her mouth popped open slightly. He held his whiskey in one hand as with the other, he grazed her exposed thigh, dragging his fingernails over her flesh.

Chrissy groaned. "Oh, god, far from over," she said as she draped her legs open wider. She waggled a finger at Tommy for him to come get her wineglass.

Tommy took a deep breath, his gaze still fixed on Jack's hand sliding closer to Chrissy's sex, the man's fingers leaving red marks on her flesh. Once he reached his wife, Tommy took the glass and moved it to a table to the side, well within reach, but also safe from being toppled. He then took Jack's glass as well, the man more interested in drinking up Chrissy than the amber liquid he had been given. When the glasses were safely perched on the table, tommy stood back to the side and out of the way, far enough to be out of sight, but close enough not to miss anything.

With their hands free, Jack and Chrissy now attacked each other with their passion, hands groping each other as their moans filled the living room. Tommy just stood to the side and watched as Jack's hand disappeared under Chrissy's skirt, shoving her legs even wider as he toyed with her wetness. Chrissy cried out, her head dropping back as she stared at Tommy while Jack fingered her.

The knot in Tommy's stomach tightened, but his cock grew harder.

CHAPTER THREE

Chrissy's moans continued to fill the room as Jack shifted her on the couch, spreading her out beside him, pushing her skirt up to her waist, so that her pussy was totally open to him. He grinned up at Tommy, smirking. "She really does have a beautiful cunt," Jack said as he pounded Chrissy's pussy with his fingers. "She always liked to be filled with thick cocks. You married a right little slut here. Too bad you can't satisfy her. Well, too bad for you, that is."

Tommy just gave a short nod, his words stuck in his throat. He had found out lately just how much Jack's words were true. When Chrissy had pried this fantasy out of Tommy, of his desire to be a little sissy cuckold, she had completely flipped from the petite, sweet wife to a hungry, insatiable hotwife, craving cocks constantly. There were times she would send pictures to him at work of some thick-cocked man she had picked up pounding into her like a little bitch. She even took videos and made Tommy jack off to them as she scolded him for being a poor lover, a sissy of a man.

"God, yes," Chrissy groaned. "I need it, need your hard cock, Jack. Please!"

Tommy squirmed where he stood as Chrissy's words hit his ears, her pleading for another man to fuck her. He chanced a glance at Jack's cock, still in his pants, and even then it was a huge bulge straining to be released. The man was huge whereas, even hard, Tommy's cock barely made a bump in his pants. He just sighed as he continued to watch.

"Is that what you need, my little tramp?" Jack asked as he toyed with Chrissy's pussy. "Why do you need my cock? Hmmm? You have a cock right over there. Isn't your little husband good enough to satisfy you?"

Inwardly, Tommy begged for Chrissy to say he satisfied her just fine, but he knew she wouldn't.

"No, I married a sissy with a tiny dick," she said, her hips pushing down onto Jack's fingers. "He can't satisfy anything with that nub of a dick he has. I need a real cock. Your cock."

"A sissy, huh?" Jack asked, and Tommy groaned again, because he knew what would happen next. "And how do I know he's a sissy?"

"Because he wears girl's panties," Chrissy said, her voice husky with passion. She turned to Tommy, her eyes glazed somewhat for the lust filling her. "Gets off on it, actually. Isn't that right, little boy? Take off your pants and show him. Show him what a sissy I married after him."

Tommy swallowed the lump in his throat, but did as his wife ordered, reaching to his pants button and opening his jeans. With his eyes closed, he slid his pants down his legs, exposing his pink panties to his wife's ex-husband, a slight wetness of his pre-cum staining the fabric.

Jack just laughed at him as he stared at Tommy. "You weren't kidding," he said. "And look at that, the little sissy is hard watching me take his wife." Jack glanced back down at Chrissy. "You really did marry a little cuckold, didn't you? I'm going to have fun with this. I can fuck the hell out of you and not have to be nagged by you. A win in my book. You were always a tasty piece of ass."

Chrissy, grabbed Jack's shoulders, pulling him closer. "I thought so. God, I've missed your cock."

Tommy watched as Jack slid his fingers from Chrissy's pussy, each digit dripping with her wetness. "Then we need to get you naked, don't we?" he asked. He then turned to Tommy, a shitty grin on his face. "Come here, sissy, and strip your wife for me. I want her completely naked." Jack slid off the couch stripping himself as he watched Tommy move over to his wife to carry out Jack's orders.

After helping Chrissy to her feet, his wife biting her bottom lips as she watched him carry out her lover's orders, Tommy reached behind her, unzipping her skirt. "Such a good sissy," she whispered as he slid her skirt down her slender legs, the aroma of her arousal strong.

"Thank you," he whispered back as he stood, pulling her shirt up her torso and off. He stared into her eyes as she stared into his as he reached behind her and unclasped her bra, sliding the straps off her shoulders and down her arms. Once she was naked, he then took her clothes in his hands and carried them off to the side, folding them as he went.

"He makes a good servant," Jack said. "Is that why you keep him around?"

Chrissy glanced over at her husband, and for the first time, Tommy saw the soft look she always gave him when she told him she loved him. "Well, it's not for his cock. He has several uses, though." She then turned back to Jack. "Maybe you'll find some of them out later."

Jack stood there, naked, his cock ramrod straight and as thick as Tommy's wrist. He shrugged as he crossed the room to where Chrissy stood. "Doesn't matter to me as long as I get to fuck his wife." He reached out, taking Chrissy's tit in his hand and pinching her nipple, drawing her downward. "Now, enough talking. I want to feel that mouth of yours on my cock like it was earlier. Kneel."

Tommy watched as his wife grinned up at her ex, lowering herself down to her knees as she reached out and took Jack's hardness in her hand. "Yes, sir," she whispered just before she licked the tip of his cock, a strand of his pre-cum stretching from the head of his dick to her tongue as she pulled away.

Tommy felt his cock throb as he watched Chrissy swallow Jack's cock as much as she could, the man's fist in her hair as he guided her back and forth on his shaft. "Now, that's a good little slut," Jack groaned as he stared at Tommy, a smirk on his face. "God, I'm going to enjoy this."

CHAPTER FOUR

Tommy stood there, staring as his wife devoured her ex's cock, her tongue twirling around the thick shaft as she pulled away to lick at Jack's balls, sucking them into her mouth as Jack kept a firm grip on her hair. Chrissy's moans escaped from around the monster cock in her mouth as Jack forced his manhood back and forth between her lips, fucking her face with hard, deep thrusts, making her choke a couple of times as he hit the back of her throat. Tommy could only watch, a knot in his stomach as he knew he would never be able to get as deep into his wife's mouth, stretching her lips as Jack's shaft did.

Jack continued to hold Chrissy's head in place as he thrust into her mouth, skull-fucking her with passionate force as the slobbering sounds of his cock going in and out of her mouth filled the room. At one point, he told Tommy to sit down in the chair and then he grabbed Chrissy by her hair, pulled her to her feet, and spun her around. Just as Tommy sat in the chair, Jack shoved Chrissy over so that her hands rested on the arms of the chair, her face inches from her husband's as her tits swayed slightly. "Watch a real man fuck the shit out of your wife's cunt," Jack practically growled as he gripped Chrissy's hips. With one thrust, he buried his cock deep into Chrissy's pussy.

Tommy watched as his wife's mouth popped open as the pleasure Jack gave her with his cock covered her face, her moans loud and hungry. Tommy could only sit there in his pink panties, his tiny cock hard, straining against the fabric as Jack pummeled into Tommy's wife, his fingers digging into her hips as he pounded her pussy with his monster cock.

Chrissy cried out, begging for Jack to fuck her harder, faster, deeper. Jack grunted as he drove in and out her cunt, the sounds of her wetness reaching Tommy's ears.

"Tell him," Jack ordered. "Tell that sissy husband of yours whose cock you prefer. Tell him who you want fucking your cunt from now on. Tell him!"

"Oh, god," Chrissy moaned, her tits swayed faster as Jack kept pumping into her pussy. "Jack's! I want Jack's cock. I need it. Miss it. Oh, god, I want him to. fuck me from now on. Only him."

Tommy could only sit there, squirming, his cock throbbing as he heard his wife's words. Jack just smirked at Tommy as he continued to pound into Tommy's wife's cunt, stretching her and making her moan as her tits swayed harder in Tommy's face. Pre-cum stained his panties as he fought the urge to grab his cock and jack off.

"Harder! Please, fuck me harder!" Chrissy moaned out. "God, I've missed your thick cock in my pussy."

"You don't miss Tommy's?" Jack asked as his hips slapped Chrissy's ass.

"God, no," she admitted. "I barely feel him when he's inside of me. I need your cock. Please! God, please."

"Do I own your pussy?" Jack demanded to know, his gaze fixed on Tommy's.

"Yes, yes!" she cried out. "It's yours. My pussy is only yours."

Tommy could see his wife's body start to shake, her back arching slightly as her head dropped down, her face inches from his cock, which she ignored.

"Oh, god!" she cried out. "Jack, I'm...Oh, god, I'm coming!"

"Watch her, sissy," Jack ordered. "Watch as another man makes your wife come on his cock. You can't do this with your pitiful little dick."

Chrissy shook her head, her long blond hair flying in all directions as her body shuddered with her orgasm. Tommy continued to fuck her, his cock thrusting into her hard from behind as he dug his fingers into her pale hips. Chrissy kept screaming, her mouth open as she shoved herself back onto the monster cock inside of her pussy.

Tommy couldn't stop himself; he came without even touching his cock, came watching another man—a man his wife didn't even like—bring her to an orgasm like she had never had with him. The white pearls of his come oozed from the fabric of his panties as he sat there and watched the scene inches from his face.

Jack just laughed at him. "What a sissy." Then the other man grunted, pulled Chrissy back hard on his cock, and emptied his load into her, filling her fertile womb with his own seed. "I hope you have my baby, cuck."

Chrissy just groaned as Tommy whimpered, his eyes wide as Jack pumped his seed into Chrissy. His wife wanted a baby, and Tommy had not been able to provide one. Now, it looked like the man she had not wanted to be married to any longer would now be the one to impregnate her. Tommy could possibly be raising another man's child.

Jack slipped out of Chrissy's cunt, spanking her ass once as he did. "Of course, if you don't want to take care of my baby, you can always eat my cum out of her."

Chrissy stood. "You have to, Tommy," she said, a look of panic on her face. "You have to eat his cum out of me. You don't want me having his baby do you?"

Tommy just bounced his gaze between the other two, not sure whether he could do what they wanted of him. Having another man fuck his wife was one thing; cleaning the man's cum from her freshly fucked pussy was quite another.

"Please, Tommy," Chrissy urged.

With a sigh, Tommy swallowed what was left of his pride and slid to the floor, resigned to even more of his wife's humiliation.

CHAPTER FIVE

As soon as Tommy was flat on his back on the floor, Chrissy straddled his face, lowering her sloppy cunt to his mouth. Tommy glanced up, soaking in his wife's open slit with her ex-husband's cum pooling at her entrance just before Chrissy sat on his face, her pussy pressed against his lips. The salty taste of Jack's cum mixed with Chrissy's wetness instantly filled Tommy's mouth.

Tommy could hear Jack laughing at him as he gripped Chrissy's thighs and drive his tongue as deep into her pussy as he could, lapping at her wetness. She ground her cunt back and forth on his mouth, covering him with juices as well as Jack's cum. It was the first time Tommy had ever ate a man's cum, even his own, and it shamed him that he was sucking up his wife's ex-husband's seed, swallowing as much of it as he could clean out of her pussy so she didn't get pregnant from her ex.

"He makes a good cleaning sissy," he heard Jack say. "We're going to make good use of him in the future."

Tommy groaned, knowing the humiliation was only beginning. Chrissy would keep bringing her ex back just to be fucked hard as she craved, and Tommy would have to endure it to see his wife satisfied. He continued to lap at her pussy, shoving his tongue as far into her passion as he could to slurp up the remnants of the fucking she just received, her moans mixed with Jack's mocking comments filling his ears. Tommy could feel her pressing on his chest as she squeezed her lover's cum into her husband's mouth, ordering him to be a good sissy and clean her out. "Make sure you get every drop. You don't want me having his baby, do you?"

After a few minutes of grinding on Tommy's face, Chrissy slid off his mouth, sitting on the floor beside him. She grinned at him, her pussy still glistening with her wetness. "Such a good little sissy," she cooed at him, her lips twisted into a mocking grin. "I think we've definitely found your place in my sex life."

Tommy groaned, hoping that his humiliation was over and Jack would leave. His hope was short-lived, however.

"You're not done, yet, sissy," Jack said, his lips twisted into a sinister smirk. "Get your ass over here and clean my cock."

Tommy stared at the other man, wide-eyed. Surely, Jack didn't expect him to suck his cock, did he?

But, he did.

"Now!" Jack demanded. "It's the least you can do for me pleasing your wife where you couldn't. Consider it a thank you." His grin grew wider as he pointed to his semi-hard member.

Tommy glanced over at Chrissy, but his wife was no help. She just sat there on the floor watching to see if he would actually do it, her eyes hopeful. *Oh, my god, she wants me to do it*. Tommy sighed at the inevitable as he flipped over to his hands and knees and crawled over to where Jack stood, hands on his hips as his cock dripped with the juices from their sex as it stood straight out, barely turning flaccid at all. Tommy's cock always deflated quickly right after he came. He was amazed the other man was still mostly hard.

He knelt in front of Jack, taking the man's cock in his hand as he brought his mouth to the tip. He felt the heat of his embarrassment warm his cheeks as he stuck his tongue out and licked the tip of Jack's cock, the juices salty to the taste.

"Suck it, bitch," Jack ordered. "Put your mouth on it and clean it from your slut wife's cunt."

Tommy heard Chrissy giggle behind him as he opened his mouth and swallowed Jack's massive cock, his tongue twirling around the thickness, running over every vein and ridge as he had watched his wife do just s short time ago. His shame slid into a hunger as he tasted his wife's pussy on the man's cock, tasted the remnants of Jack's seed from the tip of his cock. Tommy bobbed his head back and forth on Jack's manhood, savoring the feel of the way it stretched his mouth and shamed that he actually enjoyed the way it filled his mouth.

"He makes as good of a little cock sucker as he did a cleaner," he heard Jack tell Chrissy as the man's hand fell to his head, gripping his hair and shoving his face harder onto his cock until Tommy thought he would choke.

Chrissy giggled even more. "Well, at least we found a good use for the little sissy."

Tommy felt the shame warm his face even more as his cock twitched in his stained panties.

"Oh, we'll make good use of this little bitch as well as that tight cunt of yours," Jack told Chrissy. He then shoved Tommy off his cock and back onto the floor. "Now, get us something else to drink while we warm up for round two. I'm going to use both of your mouths again."

"Yes, sir," Tommy said as he hurried to carry out Jack's orders. He couldn't even look at Chrissy as he walked by his wife, shame reddening his face. She had made him the little sissy he was, and he knew he would never be able to be anything else from that point forward. Jack now owned Chrissy, and by owning her, owned Tommy. That, however, wasn't the most embarrassing part. No, what made it all worse, what embarrassed

Tommy even more, was how much the fact of being their little bitch made his cock throb. As he passed into the kitchen to fix their drinks, the sounds of Chrissy sucking Jack's cock again filling the air, Tommy only hoped they'd allow him to jack off before the night was over. Perhaps, while he was cleaning his wife's pussy or sucking Jack's cock.

Tommy's cock throbbed even more at the prospects of serving them.

CUCKOLDED BY A STRANGER

CHAPTER ONE

"I'm sorry," Kevin said as he stared at his wife, Brianna. "You did what?" He had just came in from the outside, pulling his shirt off, getting ready to change when his wife had dropped her bombshell.

Brianna shrugged her rounded shoulders, her arms crossed under her ample bosom, which was fully exposed as she stood there completely naked. "I invited someone named Tom over. He should be here shortly."

Kevin stared at his wife's nude form, still not comprehending what was happening. "Some random guy? You invited some stranger over to our house? Why?" Kevin couldn't believe what she told him. This was nothing like his demure wife. "Why in the world would you do that?"

She walked over to him, her naked hips swaying as she grinned up at him, her dark green eyes sparkling. "Isn't that what you wanted, Kevin? I saw your web browser. You forgot to close it the other night before you went out with your buddies. I saw those videos you were watching where a man comes in and fucks the hell out of some guy's wife in front of him. Didn't those videos get your little dick hard? Isn't that why I found that rag beside your desk? You use it to clean up your cum after jacking off."

He just stared at her, unsure whether he should admit it or not. She was right, of course. Those stories made his cock throb as he sat there watching them, jacking his tiny shaft off with two fingers. However, they were just videos, fantasies. He never thought to take them into his reality, which is why he never mentioned them to her. Hell, he never mentioned them to anyone.

Brianna did, however, it seemed. She patted his chest. "I take your hesitation to answer as a yes." She shrugged as she turned, her round ass beckoning his gaze to follow her as she stood naked in the middle of their living room. "So, I took the liberty of finding someone to come make your little wet dream come true." She turned back around, facing him. "It's amazing how many men are out there, eager to fuck another man's wife. It's a win for both of us, really. You get to have your fantasy come true, and I finally get a nice thick cock pounding my tight cunt. It's perfect."

Kevin swallowed the lump in his throat as he soaked in his wife's naked body. "Aren't you at least going to put something on before he gets here?"

"Why waste time?" she asked. "He's here to fuck me. Not to see a strip show. Besides, he told me to be naked, so that's exactly what he's going to get." She glared at him. "And you will sit there and watch as I finally get a real cock inside of me. You will not be a whiny little bitch as it's happening or else I'll spank your ass in front of him. Then, I'll tell everyone that you can't satisfy your wife because you're too busy jacking off to cuckold videos. Is that understood?"

Kevin swallowed again as he nodded slowly. "I understand."

"Good, now…" A knock on the front door interrupted her sentence. Her lips twisted up into a hungry grin. "Showtime. Now, be a good little boy and open the door."

Kevin just stood there staring at his wife. Surely, she didn't really expect him to welcome the man who was about to fuck her into their house.

She shooed him toward the door. "Now, or else your story gets out."

Kevin sighed as he turned toward the front door, his shoulders slumped as he resigned himself to what was about to happen. The frustrating part was how his cock was already growing inside of his jeans. Another man was about to use

Kevin's wife as his personal toy, and Kevin's cock was harder than ever while his stomach twisted into a tight knot of Christmas lights. The struggle in contradictions threatened to undo him, but he still made his way to the front door and opened it.

Standing on his front porch was the buffest black man Kevin had ever seen. His arms were thick, his chest broad, and shoulders squared. His jean-clad legs looked like mini tree trunks as he stood there waiting to be let in to fuck Kevin's wife. Kevin couldn't help it; his gaze dropped down to the man's crotch and already a huge bulge was quite evident in the front of the man's pants, already larger than Kevin's when it was fully hard. What would the neighbors think as they saw this man walk up to their front door?

"I think this is where you invite me in," the man said, his voice deep, mocking. "Your wife is expecting me."

Kevin nodded as he once again swallowed the nervousness in his throat. "Yes, sir," he stammered as he backed up a bit, admitting the man—Tom—into his home. Kevin felt his body shaking a little at what he knew he was about to be forced to endure.

Tom strode past Kevin as if the man already owned the house, owned Kevin's wife for that matter. "Damn, you look better in the naked flesh than you did in those nasty pictures you sent me," Tom said as he strode over to where Brianna stood. "Although, those photos were definitely a sweet enticement.

Kevin shut the door, staring at his wife. *She sent this man pictures of herself? How long have they been talking behind my back?*

As Tom neared Brianna, she placed her hands on his chest, her tits brushing up against him. Tom raked her body with his wolfish gaze, a smirk on his face as he soaked in what was about to be his. "I'm glad you think so," Brianna said. "I had fun taking those pictures for you. You have quite the imagination when it comes to what you wanted. It was all so hot."

Hot? What the hell have I been missing? Kevin wondered as he stood there watching the two in front of him.

Tom wrapped his thick arm around Brianna's waist, pulling her tighter against him as he leaned down and kissed her, his lips pressing hard against hers, his mouth opening as he shoved his tongue inside of her mouth, tasting her, claiming her right there in front of her husband.

Brianna instantly surrendered to the kiss, her arms going around Tom's thick neck as she ground her body agianst the hardness within his pants, moaning as they kissed. Kevin could only stand there and watch as he struggled between telling the man to get away from his wife and feeling his cock throb inside of his pants. How could he be so conflicted with how he felt?

As soon as they broke the kiss, Brianna started to strip the man she had invited over, the man she had never truly met before except for some online chat and picture swapping. Kevin just stared as she pulled Tom's shirt over his head and then immediately went for his belt buckle. Holding his breath, Kevin watched as his wife pulled the other man's pants down his legs, exposing the longest, thickest cock Kevin could imagine.

Brianna grinned as she glanced down at the swollen black cock in front of her, reaching out and stroking it in her tiny white hand. "Now, that's a cock," she cooed. She then glanced over at her husband. "I'm going to enjoy riding this. I'll feel like a virgin again taking it inside my pussy."

Kevin could only nod as he swallowed yet again.

CHAPTER TWO

Kevin watched as the other man pulled Brianna over to the recliner, sitting down and dragging her down beside him as he opened his legs, his massive cock poking straight up. With his arm around Brianna, Tom glanced over at Kevin. "Get down here and suck my cock," he ordered. "Now."

Kevin stared at the other man a moment, confused. *He doesn't really think I'm going to suck his cock, does he? That wasn't what Brianna told me.* He glanced over at his wife, hoping she would tell him not to do it. However, when he saw the smirk on his wife's face, he knew she would not come to his rescue.

"Listen, you little bitch," Tom said, growling. "I'm here to satisfy your wife because obviously you can't. You're going to help with that. Now get down here and start sucking a real cock before I make you."

With a sigh, Kevin walked over to the two of them, resigned to his fate, and dropped to his knees between the other man's legs. He glanced up, hoping that Tom only blustered in front of Brianna and changed his mind, but the other man was already pulling Brianna to him, kissing her again as he pulled at one of her nipples, stretching her large breast a little, pinching it as she moaned.

Kevin took a deep breath and lowered his mouth to the thick, dark cock in front of him. He had never thought about sucking another man's cock before, but he had read that most cuckolds did it, had watched it happen in the videos he jacked off to when Brianna wasn't home. This was his new role, fluffer, and quite possibly cleaner as his wife enjoyed cocks the size she hadn't felt since college.

Running his tongue over the other man's cock, he tasted the pre-cum at the tip as the sounds of his wife's moans reached his ears. He swallowed Tom's cock as Brianna pushed against him as the other man massaged and devoured her titties. Kevin could imagine the other man's mouth on her nipples, could hear him sucking on the large globes as Brianna squirmed and moaned beside him. From the corner of his eye, he saw Tom's hand between Brianna's thighs, stroking her clit. Kevin felt his cock throb as he continued to suck the large rod in his mouth, bobbing his head up and down on the thick shaft imaging it soon pummeling his wife's cunt. Soon, he felt Tom's hand on his head and then his wife's as they shoved his head down on the cock in his mouth faster, forcing him to take more into his mouth, sucking faster as Tom thrust upward hitting the back of Kevin's throat.

"Did you make it good and hard for me, my little bitch?" Brianna asked. "I want it nice and solid when I climb on top of it."

Kevin bobbed up and down on it a couple of more times before sliding his mouth from the hard shaft, licking the tip as he pulled away, and glancing up at his wife. "It's hard, ma'am," he said, his voice soft as his face burned red from the humiliation of sucking her lover's cock to prepare it for her.

"Move back," Tom said as he dragged Brianna over his lap, making her straddle him.

Kevin slid back on the floor, sitting there as his wife eased her pussy over the dark cock between her legs. She slid back and forth on it a few times, groaning as Tom pulled her tit into his mouth again, his mouth wide as he devoured her large globe, swallowing her aureole whole. Brianna groaned as she rode the man's hardness, and after a while, Kevin watched as she reached down between them and guided Tom's cock into her pussy. She moaned loudly as she lowered herself down onto the thickness of manmeat spearing her open. Tom could only stare as he watched the black cock disappear into his wife's wetness. Then Brianna rode Tom's cock with a feverish grind, her round ass bouncing, her flesh rolling as she slid back and forth, fucking the stranger, her hands gripping Tom's shoulders. Every once in a while, Tom would pull her down, kissing her some more before returning to her tits, sucking her swollen nipples into his mouth.

Brianna kept grinding, her moans filling the room as she rode back and forth on the massive monster of a cock inside of her. Tom had his hands on her hips gripping her so he could control how fast or slow she went, changing the pace up as Brianna's tits swung in his face.

"God, your cock is so thick," she groaned, her eyes closed as she slid faster on Tom's cock. "I've missed being this full."

"Slut, I love how tight your white pussy is," Tom said as he watched her sliding back and forth on his dick. "God, white women are so fucking horny and ready to be opened up."

"God, yes, please, take that pussy," Brianna cried out. "You feel so good."

Kevin felt the twisting in his gut at his wife's words, at the way the other man took her, used her. Pleased her. Pleased her in ways Kevin could never do.

"I want to take you from behind like a little bitch," Tom told her as he slapped her ass. "Get up, slut."

Brianna slowed her grinding as she bit her lower lip, grinning. She then slid back off Tom, her pussy glistening with her wetness as she stood.

Tom lifted himself off the chair, his cock wet with Brianna's juices. He pointed to the chair. "Bend over, slut," he ordered.

"Yes, sir," Brianna replied with a sultry grin. She bent over, her hands on the seat of the chair, her round ass up in the air begging for Tom's cock.

Kevin watched as Tom gripped Brianna's hips, his cock poised at her slick entrance. "Do you want it, bitch?" he asked her. "Are you ready to feel a real man's cock?"

"Oh, god, yes," Brianna groaned as Kevin watched her push her ass back to Tom's cock. "Fuck me, please. Shove that monster into my cunt. I need it. God, I need it after putting up with my husband's tiny dick for so long."

Tom dug his fingers into her pale flesh and with one thrust, buried himself into her soaked cunt. Briana's mouth popped open as she cried out, her body going tense "Yes!" she screamed.

CHAPTER THREE

Brianna's cries hit Kevin's ears, twisting the knot in his stomach as his cock dripped pre-cum. The living room filled with Brianna's whimpers and moans as well as the sound of Tom's hips smacking against her round ass. She shoved back on his cock, matching Tom's thrusts as he drove into her over and over, faster, harder. Soon, Brianna's face was pressed into the chair, her hands bracing her up as her whole body rocked under Tom's onslaught.

Kevin felt his tiny cock throbbing in his pants as he sat on the floor, watching his wife get the shit fucked out of her. He couldn't believe how long Tom lasted. Kevin would have already shot his wimpy load into her and be snoring by now. No wonder Brianna was groaning so loudly. This was more than she had between her legs since she married Kevin, and that humilated him even more.

Then, Tom slowed, shifting a little. Brianna's breathing took on a slower pace, her moans shifting to a lower purr, and Kevin knew the other man was pushing his cock into her ass. Kevin watched as his wife's body tightened, bracing for the intrusion into her back door. She had never allowed Kevin to take her there, and here she was, giving Tom, a man she just met, free access to her most virgin of holes.

Tom pushed in slowly at first, his hands gripping her waist as he entered her, giving her time to adjust to the full feeling in her tight ass. Then as soon as he eased his cock past the tight ring in her ass, Tom picked up the pace, gripping her tighter as he slammed into her over and over, making her body jump, her cries grow louder.

"God, yes, my ass, take my ass," Brianna screamed as she shoved herself back onto Tom's cock. "Oh god, it hurts so good. I feel it splitting me open. God, yes! More. Please give me more."

Tom obliged, slamming into her over and over, his cock spreading her ass as he shoved her into the chair with the force of his pounding. Brianna was out of control with her whimpers, her whole body shaking from the assault to her ass, and yet, she still begged for more.

Kevin wasn't sure how long Tom continued to take her ass, but eventually, he slid his cock out of her tight back door, making her shudder as he pulled her back into a standing position. He moved her to the side as he sat back down in the chair, and then, he pulled her down on top of him, only instead of his cock going into her pussy as Kevin expected, he made her slide her ass back down on him.

Brianna's eyes widened, but she turned and lowered her ass to his cock. Kevin watched as Tom held his thick, black cock in one hand, guiding it into Brianna's dark hole as she slid down onto him. She bit her lower lip, her eyes closed as her ass swallowed the monster penetrating her once more, her hands gripping Tom's powerful thighs.

"Good girl," Tom said as he stared at Brianna's perfect ass. "Now, fuck me with that fat ass of yours."

Brianna groaned. "Oh, god, yes, sir. I'll try."

"You'll do it, slut," Tom ordered as he gripped her waist.

Brianna whimpered as she started to slide up and down on the thick cock buried in her ass, slowly at first, and then picking up speed as she moaned with pleasure.

Kevin watched as his wife devoured Tom's cock in her ass, riding it as opposed to being fucked. She was the one doing it now, riding that monster cock, giving her lover pleasure with her tight ass.

Tom then reached around and spread Brianna's legs, opening her pussy up to his fingers. Brianna spread her legs as wide as she could while keeping his cock in her ass, and Tom started to toy with her clit.

Brianna's eyes popped open, her mouth forming a wide O as she groaned out even louder. "Oh, god!"

Tom continued to finger her clit, rubbing his fingers up and down on her as he shoved his cock up into her ass, pinning her down on top of him. Brianna could only sit there and take it, his fingers strumming her into wild abandon as his cock pegged her from underneath. She just sat there, taking it all as she whimpered and mewled at what Tom did to her body.

Then the other man looked over at Kevin. "Get over here and eat her pussy," he ordered. "I want to feel your fingers in her cunt as well. Do it."

Kevin rushed to get between his wife's legs, the sight of Tom's cock sliding between her ass cheeks as her pussy spread open before him making his cock twitch. Quickly, Kevin lowered his mouth to his wife's pussy, running his tongue up between her folds, tasting her wetness which gushed from her cunt. As he sucked on her clit, swallowing it like a small cock, he shoved two fingers into her pussy, curving them slightly so they touched the sweet spot at the top of her cunt.

She cried out as he fingered her, his mouth sucking on her clit. Tom shoved upward into her ass even more, thrusting slowly as he moved under her. Kevin could feel the man's cock rubbing his fingers through Brianna's pussy walls, knew how full his wife must feel with both holes filled and being used.

"God, yes," she screamed out. "More, finger me faster, you little bitch."

Kevin obeyed, shoving his fingers in and out of her wetness as her juices flowed down his fingers, coating his knuckles. He tongued her pussy lips, finding it harder now to keep his mouth suctioned to her clit as Tom fucked her ass.

"Yes!" Brianna screamed again. "Oh, god, Tom, I'm...oh, god, Tom, I'm coming."

And Kevin felt his wife's body shudder around his head as her thighs clamped down onto his face, her ass sucking on the cock buried inside of it. Her body rippled with her orgasm as she held Kevin in place until he thought he would suffocate from the pressure.

Finally, she relaxed, her chest heaving with her heavy breaths. "God, that was awesome," she sighed as she settled back onto Tom's chest, his cock still deep in her ass. She glanced down at her husband. "Good, boy." She motioned to the other couch with a tilt of her head. "You may go sit down now and pull out that cock of yours. You deserve some reward, and Tom deserves a good laugh."

Kevin nodded as he sucked in a breath, shame flaming across his face knowing the other man would see how pathetic his cock was. Still, he obeyed, somehow eager for the humiliation.

CHAPTER FOUR

As he stood in front of the couch, Kevin unbuttoned and unzipped his pants before sliding them down his legs, his tiny cock poking out as soon as it was free. With a deep breath bracing for what he knew would come next, he turned and sat down, his pants around his ankles.

Brianna grinned over at him. "See what I mean?" she asked Tom as she leaned back into him. "See how tiny that dick is?"

While he roamed his hands over Brianna's body, squeezing her breasts and stomach, his cock still buried in her ass, Tom glanced over at Kevin a smirk on his lips. "That is tiny. Did he even get past your entrance?"

Brianna laughed as Kevin started to stroke his inferior dick, barely needing two fingers to do it. "Barely," she said. "He came on my folds more than he ever came inside of me." She shook her head. "Pathetic."

Tom squeezed her back against him as he nuzzled her neck. "Don't you worry, baby," he said as he kissed the side of her face. "Tom here has plenty of cock for you, and I'll give it to you every day." As if to prove his point, he thrust upward, jamming his cock deeper into her ass.

Brianna moaned even more, which made Kevin grip his cock harder, stroking it feverishly, his breathing heavy in his own ears. He couldn't take his eyes off his wife as Tom thrusted into her from underneath, shoving his massive cock into her ass, making her cry out. Harder, he pulled Brianna down onto his shaft as he shoved his hips upward. Brianna added to the motion, bouncing up and down on Tom's cock as her whimpers filled the room.

Then Tom lifted her off his cock as he stood, taking her with him. He spun her around, shoving her over the arm of the chair in a rush as he grabbed her hips and drove his cock back into her sopping wet pussy. Brianna screamed, begging for more of his manhood, begging the stranger to own her body, claim it.

Kevin couldn't take anymore and felt his tiny dick twitch in his grip as thin ropes of cum spewed from the tip, coating his fingers and dribbling to his stomach. He groaned, his gaze still locked on the others as Tom continued to drill into Brianna's pussy.

"God, yes!" she screamed. "Give me that cock. Please! I want it."

"I'm going to come in that white pussy, slut," Tom growled.

Kevin felt his eyes widen at the words. "No!" he cried out. "Not in her cunt. Don't come inside of her. She's not on birth control."

"I don't care," Brianna cried out. "I want it. I want that cum inside of me."

Tom grunted as he pulled her back, pinning her to his cock as he emptied his seed into her dripping cunt, filling her with his fertile seed.

Kevin could only sit there and stare, his cock still in his hand as the stranger filled his wife with cum, possibly even impregnating her. He felt the grip to his chest as the thought of raising a black man's baby filled him. What would their family think? They would know it wasn't Kevin's. The shame filled him.

Brianna just groaned, however, wiggling her ass back onto Tom's massive rod.

When Tom slipped out, he turned and sat back in the recliner as Brianna slowly stood straight. She grinned over at Kevin. "Get on the floor," she ordered.

He gave her a quizzical look. "What? Why?"

"Because you have to clean me with that tongue of yours if you don't want me having his baby," she informed him. "You don't want me to get pregnant, do you?"

Kevin groaned, but did as he was told and slid to lie flat on the floor.

Brianna sauntered over to him, stepping to each side of his face as she lowered her cum-filled pussy to his waiting mouth. "Make sure you get every last drop," she said as she placed her pussy on his mouth, sliding her messy folds back and forth over his mouth.

Kevin could hear Tom smirk as cum dripped from Brianna's pussy into Kevin's mouth. He ran his tongue up her gaping slit, shoving it inside and lapping up the other man's seed, doing his best to get every last drop of the salty substance. He could feel his wife squeezing, pushing more cum out of her pussy and into his mouth as he tongued her, his arms out flat at his sides as she ground on his face, moaning. "Such a good little cleaner," she said as she slid back and forth on his face.

Once Brianna thought her pussy clean enough, she pushed herself back to her feet, and then moved over to sit beside Tom again.

Kevin lifted himself into a sitting position, but he should have known his chores weren't over.

Brianna grinned at him as she pointed to Tom's still hard cock dripping with their mixed juices. "Come on," she said. "Tom needs you to clean his cock as well."

Kevin sighed but crawled over to where the others sat, surrendering to whatever other humiliation his wife had in store for him.

CHAPTER FIVE

Kevin crawled across the floor, keeping his focus on Tom's cock so he didn't have to see the expressions on his wife's face. She had taken complete advantage of what she found on his computer, using it to finally get the cock she wanted and humiliating him in the process. He didn't blame her. She had remained sexually unsatisfied their entire marriage. The sad part was that Kevin was still turned on by it all and even wanted more.

He leaned in, his hands going to Tom's thighs as he took the other man's cock into his mouth, tasting Brianna's pussy and ass all over the man's thick shaft. Tom just laughed as Kevin worked his mouth up and down, lapping around the sides to make sure he cleaned every bit of their sex from Tom's cock. Already Kevin could hear the other two kissing again, their lust far from abated.

After running his tongue all around Tom's rod, he pulled his mouth off and sucked on the man's heavy balls, running his tongue over the hard ridges, sucking the balls into his mouth and cleaning them of Brianna's juices, the musky aroma filling his nostrils.

When he was done, he simply sat back on his heels and waited for further instructions, watching as Tom kneaded Brianna's chest as the two of them made out. Kevin would never be able to look at the recliner without seeing what he saw now. His wife had cuckolded him with someone she had just met online, and Kevin knew it was only the beginning.

As the kiss broke, Brianna turned and smiled at Kevin. "Go start the shower and make sure there are two towels waiting for us in the bathroom. We'll be right there."

Kevin nodded. "Yes, ma'am." Pushing himself to his feet, he moved to carry out her orders, her giggles in his ears as Tom went back to her tits.

Once they joined him in the bathroom, steam coming from the shower, Brianna patted his cheek, smiling. "You may go now," she told him, and as he stepped out of the bathroom, she closed the door on him, leaving him to wonder what would happen on the other side.

It didn't take long before he heard the sounds of Tom fucking Brianna again coming from the closed door. Kevin sighed as he turned to go to the kitchen. *They're going to need something to drink,* he thought as he surrendered to his new life. *I better get to it.*

Avery Rowan's Books

On Amazon

Taken While Camping

Served Picnic Style

Taken in the Woods

Taken by the Fire

Her Swimming Holes

Taken While Camping Box Set

Adventures in Swinging

Venturing Out

Play Date

After Party

Chelsea's Date

House Party

Darren's Surprise

Swinging Neighbors

Swinging Vacation

Adventures in Swinging Volume 1

Cuckold Stories

From the Front Seat

His Booty-Call Wife

About the Author

Avery Rowan has had a titillating fantasy life and, thankfully for us, Avery has decided to share some of those stories with us. Avery's stories contain strong characters, wild adventures, and a high level of steaminess. While each has a happy ending, they also leave you breathing heavy and wishing your lover or battery-operated-boyfriend was near at hand.

Avery lives along the beach in sunny Florida, basking in the sun's rays while the rolling waves provide a soothing white noise to the writing process. When not writing, Avery is with family and friends, getting the most out of this life, just like the characters in Avery's stories. Life is to be lived and savored, not shied away from, so break out of the norms and grab all you can get out of it.

For up-to-date news on Avery's latest releases, book signing events in your area, and giveaways, follow Avery's newsletter - http://eepurl.com/dCBBwP

Also follow Avery at:

Amazon Page ~ https://www.amazon.com/Avery-Rowan/e/B07G7HTBKS

Website ~ https://sandyshorespub.wixsite.com/averyrowan

Facebook Page ~ https://www.facebook.com/averyrowanauthor/